VIRTUAL UNIVERSITY PRESS

H. P. Lovecraft's

At the Mountains of Madness

ACADEMIC EDITION

With Introduction, Author Bio, Study Guide & Chapter Quizzes

Abby Leigh Hunter, Editor

At the Mountains of Madness: Academic Edition

First Edition: August 20, 2020

This edition is part of a classic literature series designed for classroom use by English, literature, and writing students, as well as for the enjoyment of casual readers. It includes an Editor's Foreword with Author Bio, a study guide with chapter summaries and discussion prompts, and chapter-based quizzes to help readers grasp important concepts, characters, and events in the story.

Single copies of this book may be obtained in e-book, paperback, and hardcover editions from online booksellers and brick-and-mortar bookstores using the ISBNs below to locate the desired format. College bookstores and retailers may place wholesale orders through Ingram Content Group using Ingram's iPage order system.

ISBN Numbers

978-1-64399-027-9	Kindle digital edition
978-1-64399-031-6	EPUB digital edition
978-1-64399-028-6	Paperback (Amazon.com)
978-1-64399-029-3	Retail Paperback (Ingram)
978-1-64399-030-9	Retail Hardcover (Ingram)

Virtual University Press

Website:	https//books.vu.org
Email:	Editor@VU.org
Phone:	(805) 888-2900
Fax:	(805) 702-2700

Table of Contents

Editor's Foreword

This Academic Edition contains the full text of H. P Lovecraft's novella, *At the Mountains of Madness*. It also includes this Editor's Foreword, which provides historical context on the book and insights into the author's life; a study guide with chapter summaries and discussion prompts; and a set of chapter-based, multiple-choice quizzes. The book is intended for classroom use by English, literature, and writing students, as well as casual readers in search of a great story. It is arranged in two sections: Lovecraft's story is presented in the first half, and the study guide/ workbook follows. Answers to the chapter quizzes are given at the back of the book.

This edition also has an interactive component, giving readers free access to a "virtual classroom" devoted to *At the Mountains of Madness* on the Virtual University Press website. This e-learning environment offers an assortment of educational features, including interactive quizzes with real-time scoring; a Web Resources section with curated videos and further study materials; and a Vocabulary Guide to help readers grasp uncommon words used throughout the story. The classroom can be accessed online at: https://books.vu.org/titles/lovecraft_atmm

Written in 1931, Lovecraft's masterpiece, *At the Mountains of Madness,* was submitted for publication to *Weird Tales* magazine but rejected because the editor thought it was too long. Five years later, it was serialized in the February, March, and April 1936 issues of *Astounding Stories of Super-Science.* Lovecraft was paid $315 for the novella, which was the most he had ever earned from his writing. But the story was harshly edited and angered Lovecraft, who called *Astounding Stories* editor F. Orlin Tremaine "that god-damn'd dung of a hyena."

Inspiration for this novella is thought to have come from Lovecraft's great interest in Antarctica, one of the last unexplored regions on earth. Lin Carter, author of *A Look Behind the Cthulhu Mythos,* suggests it was Lovecraft's extreme sensitivity to cold temperatures that brought the story to life, and he noted: "The pages of *Madness* convey the blighting, blasting, stifling sensation caused by sub-zero temperatures in a way that even Poe could not suggest."

The story opens with a narrator (later identified as Professor Dyer, a geology professor at the fictional Miskatonic University in Massachusetts), recounting the details of his ill-fated expedition to the Antarctic. Dyer says he doesn't want to tell the story but feels compelled to do so, hoping it will dissuade another planned expedition from visiting the Antarctic and encountering the calamities that befell his own group as they unearthed shocking evidence of an ancient alien civilization.

Dyer tells of the gruesome carnage that doomed his Antarctic expedition in September 1930. His team had planned to deploy a technologically advanced drilling tool developed by engineering professor Frank Pabodie, who had signed on to the expedition. After a long sea journey, they finally reached land. A prospecting group led by Dyer's colleague, Professor Lake, broke off from the main camp and set out to explore a site 300 miles away. Once there, Lake made extraordinary discoveries, including fossils and irrefutable evidence of an alien civilization that had inhabited the Antarctic continent eons ago. His men unearthed the remains of fourteen mysterious life forms, obviously of extraterrestrial origin. As Lake relayed news of his astounding finds to the main expedition, Dyer made plans to fly out to Lake's camp as soon as the winds permit safe travel.

The next morning, the base camp loses contact with Lake. Dyer and a graduate student (Danforth) load a plane with basic supplies and set out on a search mission. When they arrive at the isolated outpost, they find that Lake and his men have been killed, their bodies viciously mutilated, and the sledge dogs have been slaughtered. One of the men, one dog, and some supplies are missing from the site of the bloody carnage.

Dyer and Danforth undertake an aerial survey to determine what might have happened to Lake's camp and hopefully locate the missing man. Their search leads them to the ruins of an ancient city built by aliens and evidently abandoned millions of years ago. They refer to the extraterrestrial creatures as the "Old Ones" or "Elder Things." Further exploration reveals that the city was built using biological entities, called shoggoths, which the aliens created and bred to provide slave labor.

At times during their existence on earth, the Old Ones lived on land, at other times in the sea. They waged great wars with other extraterrestrials and had to contend with civil unrest from their own shoggoth, who began to develop free will and a rebellious spirit. The Old Ones recorded their history in meticulously engraved wall sculptures which Dyer and Danforth encounter throughout the abandoned city.

The men eventually discover the truth behind the fate of Prof. Lake's camp and push forward with their investigation, driven by intellectual curiosity. They encounter huge albino penguins at a chasm in a towering mountain, and nearby, they find the bodies of several Old Ones who had been alive very recently but slaughtered by an unknown foe. When they stumble upon an enormous, bubbling black mass, they assume that it too had been wounded and was dying. But the monster is still alive, and the men realize that it is one of the murderous shoggoth depicted in the Old Ones' wall murals. They flee in terror, the hideous creature in hot pursuit.

They manage to reach their plane safely and escape from the horrors of the alien city. Once on board, Dyer takes the controls because Danforth is so badly shaken that he cannot fly the plane. As the craft ascends, Danforth looks back and sees something that pushes him over the edge into madness. Even after returning to America and undergoing psychiatric treatment, he refuses to discuss the horror he saw when he looked back, although he hinted that it was some kind of mirage.

Now, years later, Dyer learns that a new expedition is planning a trek to the Antarctic, and he decides that he must make them aware of his own disastrous expedition. He believes his story will convince them that no one must ever return to the ice-bound alien city at the world's southern pole—the fate of mankind hangs in the balance.

About the Author

Howard Phillips Lovecraft, better known to sci-fi fans and readers as H.P. Lovecraft, was an American horror, fantasy, and science fiction writer. He wrote under his own name as well as the pseudonyms Abdul Alhazred, Lewis Theobald, Humphrey Littlewit, Ward Phillips, and Edward Softly. Born in Providence, Rhode Island, on August 20, 1890, he was the only child of parents who put off marrying until their thirties, an unusually late start at that time. Although relatively affluent, the death of his father when Lovecraft was three left the family struggling. His father, Winfield Scott Lovecraft, a traveling salesman, had suffered an episode of acute psychosis in a Chicago hotel room while on a business trip in 1893. He was brought back to Rhode Island and spent the next five years committed in the psych ward at Butler Hospital in Providence until his death in 1898. Medical records show that he had been "doing and saying strange things" in the months leading up to his mental breakdown, and it is widely believed that he was suffering from tertiary syphilis. Winfield's cause of death was officially listed as general paresis, a euphemism for late-stage syphilis. Growing up and as an adult, Lovecraft refused to accept that his father had died of syphilis, insisting that he had suffered from insomnia and overwork, which eventually took its toll.

H.P. Lovecraft at age 6, circa 1900

After his father's death, Lovecraft was raised by his mother, Sarah Susan, nicknamed Susie. They shared a home with two maternal aunts, Lillian and Annie, and his maternal grandparents, Whipple and Robie. According to family accounts, the boy and his mother were quite close. Lovecraft later recalled that his father's death had left her "permanently stricken with grief."

Whipple became a father figure to Lovecraft and had a major influence on the boy's intellectual development, teaching him to read and write by the age of three, and introducing him to classical literature and English poetry. Lovecraft would later describe his grandfather as being "the center of my entire universe." Whipple told bedtime stories featuring weird tales of "winged creatures" that made "deep moaning sounds," which would become recurring themes in Lovecraft's writings years later. Prominent literary influences from his childhood included *One Thousand and One Nights*, a gift from his mother; Ovid's *Metamorphoses*; and *Age of Fable* by Thomas Bulfinch.

Growing up, Lovecraft was often ill, physically and psychologically, and he had an unruly disposition, all of which contributed to him missing many days of school. But during his days at home, he read voraciously and developed a fascination with astronomy and the writings of Edgar Allen Poe. By age six, he was considered a prodigy. At the age of seven, he was writing poetry and rewriting verses from the *Odyssey* and other great mythology classics. It was around this time that he learned Santa Claus was a myth, and he angrily demanded, "Why is God not equally a myth?"

At twelve, Lovecraft began writing and publishing *Rhode Island Journal of Astronomy,* reflecting his love for the night skies and his imaginings of what might lie beyond. He not only wrote the content but printed copies of the magazine on a mimeograph machine, producing at least seventy-five issues. His prized possession as a young boy was a telescope.

In 1900, Lovecraft's grandfather suffered a series of financial setbacks, and he had to let the domestic help go. In 1904, Whipple's main business collapsed. A few months later, at age seventy, he died of a stroke. His death left the family in dire financial straits. His mother could not afford to maintain the family home, and they moved into a small apartment. Lovecraft was deeply affected by these changes. He would later describe this as one of the darkest times in his life, and he said that he had contemplated suicide. That fall, he began high school, where he excelled and made a small circle of friends; but he suffered repeated bouts of depression and instability that caused him to miss many days of school. During this period, he wrote the first two stories in the genre for which he would become famous decades after his death: *The Alchemist* and *The Beast in the Cave.*

In 1908, the year that Lovecraft was to graduate from high school, he suffered some unspecified malady that proved to be debilitating and life-changing. It's not clear whether his illness was physical or psychological, or a combination of both. In a letter, he described it as "a sort of breakdown...a nervous collapse," which he blamed on the stress of attending school. In another letter concerning the events of that year, he declared: "I was and am prey to intense headaches, insomnia, and general nervous weakness which prevents my continuous application to anything."

According to a classmate's account, Lovecraft experienced painful tics, and "he would be sitting in his chair, and he'd suddenly up and jump." Harold Brobst, a psychology professor who had reviewed the details of Lovecraft's affliction, suggested that chorea, a condition characterized by involuntary spasms and tremors, was the probable cause. Lovecraft himself acknowledged that he suffered from episodes of chorea as a child. Brobst further conjectured that Lovecraft's 1908 breakdown was caused by severe depression. In another letter Lovecraft wrote about the episode, he confided that he "could hardly bear to see or speak to anyone," and he "liked to shut out the world by pulling down dark shades and using artificial light." Although he had planned to attend Brown University, he never graduated high school or pursued a higher education, a failing that was a source of disappointment and shame throughout his life.

For the next five years, Lovecraft and his mother struggled financially. He evidently had become painfully self-conscious and introverted. A neighbor and close family friend, Clara Hess, said that Susie had once told her the boy was "being so hideous that he hid from everyone and did not like to walk on the streets where people could gaze on him." Clara argued that this wasn't true, but Susie maintained her opinion. At times, neighbors complained of loud arguments coming from the Lovecraft home, but a friend acquainted with their habits said that Susie and her son were loudly reciting Shakespeare, which was one of their favorite pastimes.

In 1911, Lovecraft acquired a new hobby of penning letters to the editors of pulp fiction magazines. He dabbled at opinion writing for the next two years. In 1913, he wrote a letter criticizing Fred Jackson, a popular writer for the pulp magazine *Argosy.* He lambasted Jackson's stories as "trivial, effeminate, and, in places, coarse," and he referred to his characters in disparaging racist terms, sparking a year-long feud in the Letters to the Editor section between Lovecraft, Jackson, and a few of their followers. The war of words caught the attention of Edward Daas, editor of the United Amateur Press Association (UAPA). He invited Lovecraft and Russell to join the organization, and both writers accepted.

During the next decade, Lovecraft devoted himself to amateur writing, and he worked his way up through the ranks of the UAPA, first serving as a committee chairman, then as vice-president in 1915. Two years later, he was elected president. He frequently took fellow writers to task for using relaxed language and "Americanisms" that deviated from formal English.

Lovecraft published his first short story, *The Alchemist,* in the UAPA journal in 1916. He began writing more fiction, encouraged by W. Paul

Cook, a member of the organization who would become a lifelong friend. He subsequently published *The Tomb,* which he acknowledged followed the style of Edgar Allen Poe, who was a major inspiration for Lovecraft. In 1917, he enlisted in the Army to support the U.S. effort in World War I. He passed the physical exam but never completed his enlistment, confiding to a friend that his mother was adamantly opposed to him joining the military, and she had "threatened to go to any lengths, legal or otherwise, if I do not reveal all the ills which unfit me for the army."

Lovecraft in 1915 (age 25)

In 1918, Susie suffered a partial nervous breakdown and moved in with her sister Lillian. Years later, in 1948, her friend, Clara Hess, revealed in an interview that in the weeks leading up to the breakdown, Susie had been hallucinating "weird and fantastic creatures that rushed out from behind buildings and from dark corners." Hess also stated that on one occasion, she had witnessed Susie in a delirious state of confusion and did not know where she was. Shortly after New Year's in 1919, Susie was committed to Butler Hospital, ironically, where her husband had been committed.

Lovecraft was distraught over his mother's condition and told a friend that his life "seems of little value," and he wished that "it might terminate." After visiting with his mother several times at the hospital, he realized that she would never be released, and he seemed to make a conscious decision to move on with his life. He became more outgoing, participating in social events and attending writers' conferences with friends. He met several writers during this time who would become lifelong friends and confidants.

In 1920, Lovecraft published the first horror stories that would eventually become the foundation of his Cthulhu Mythos. The next year, his mother died at Butler Hospital following gall bladder surgery, and the news sent Lovecraft spiraling into another bout of dark depression. Nevertheless, he continued to attend amateur writers' conferences, and at a convention in July, 1921, he met Sonia Greene, whom he would marry three years later.

The newlyweds faced financial difficulties from the start. Lovecraft's aunts disapproved of Sonia, so he moved in to her apartment in Brooklyn, hopeful that his writing career would flourish. Greene would later confide that he was "an adequate lover" but quite shy, and she always had to take the initiative in every aspect of their relationship. She was evidently a good cook, as Lovecraft's weight ballooned up to 200 pounds in a short time.

It was during this year in New York that Lovecraft met several influential writers who became friends and encouraged him to begin submitting his stories to the magazine *Weird Tales*. Some of his stories were accepted for publication, although the pay was paltry and left the newly married couple struggling to make ends meet. In 1925, on New Year's Day, Sonia moved to Ohio for a job. Lovecraft remained in New York, moving out of the apartment he had shared with Sonia and into a smaller apartment in a less affluent Brooklyn neighborhood.

A year later, Sonia's business failed. Then, she lost what remained of her assets in a bank failure; and to make matters worse, she fell ill. Lovecraft made an effort to support her, taking odd jobs, but his lack of training and experience only qualified him for low-wage, clerical positions. Edward Baird, the publisher of *Weird Tales*, offered him a job as editor to help make ends meet, but it required that he relocate to Chicago, so he declined.

Fate took another cruel turn when Baird was replaced by Farnsworth Wright, a writer whom Lovecraft had repeatedly criticized. Lovecraft continued to submit stories to the magazine, but Wright rejected most of them. Ironically, after Lovecraft's death, Wright published many of the stories that he had previously rejected.

Sonia continued to struggle, moving from Cleveland to Cincinnati and back to Cleveland, constantly traveling for her job. While that was going on in Ohio, Lovecraft's Brooklyn apartment was burglarized, and everything he owned except the clothes he wore was stolen. In August, 1925, he wrote *The Horror at Red Rock* and then *He,* in which the narrator of the story declares: "My coming to New York was a mistake; for whereas I had looked for poignant wonder and inspiration, I had found instead only a sense of horror and oppression which threatened to master, paralyze, and annihilate me." His next writing project, *The Call of Cthulhu,* painted a dark picture of the world and of humanity's insignificance.

Sonia Greene (undated)

Despite her own troubles, Sonia managed to send Lovecraft a small allowance, which he used to move to a run-down, one-room apartment in a rough part of Brooklyn. He subsisted there for about a year, losing more than 40 pounds of his weight. Finally, in 1926, he gave up on New York and returned to Providence.

The next ten years, which would be the last decade of Lovecraft's life, was the most prolific of his writing career. He produced most of the stories for which he is known today, including *At the Mountains of Madness* and *The Dream-Quest of Unknown Kadath.* He took on a quite a bit of work as an editor and did ghostwriting as well, including *Winged Death* and *The*

Mound. Harry Houdini, the world-renowned magician, was one of his clients and profusely complimented Lovecraft's work. Houdini introduced him to the publisher of a major newspaper syndicate, but before plans for a joint effort got off the ground, Houdini died.

Despite the hard work Lovecraft invested in his writing, and despite his vivid imagination and extraordinary talent, he remained quite poor, and his career never advanced beyond the obscurity of writing stories for pulp magazines for a pittance and editing the works of others. His close friends suggested that he sabotaged his own success by his frequent bouts of instability and depression, and by a fear of criticism, which would send him into dark moods and withdrawal. When a story was rejected once, he gave up on it. When he wrote a story with potential for commercial success, such as *The Shadow Over Innsmouth*, he made no effort to market it. And when a book publisher once asked if he had a novel available to publish, which he did—*The Case of Charles Dexter Ward*—he never typed and submitted it.

Several years after he returned to Rhode Island, he and wife Sonia, who had lived apart for years, agreed to an amicable divorce. Sonia moved to California in 1933. Trusting Lovecraft's assurances that he had signed and filed the documents to finalize their divorce (which he had not), she remarried in 1936. That same year, Lovecraft was diagnosed with intestinal cancer. He died on March 15, 1937 at the age of 46, broke, alone, and unknown.

Today, Lovecraft's writing is embraced in popular culture, and he is a cult icon for his Cthulhu Mythos, a series of loosely connected writings. His works, which have been given their own sub-genre of Lovecraftian Horror, have profoundly influenced or inspired a wide variety of novels, movies, music, and comic series. In fact, Lovecraft is now recognized as one of history's greatest horror writers. Novelist Stephen King told American Heritage magazine: "Now that time has given us some perspective on his work, I think it is beyond doubt that H.P. Lovecraft has yet to be surpassed as the twentieth century's greatest practitioner of the classic horror tale." Likewise, many other writers have recognized Lovecraft as an important influence, including Clive Barker, Neil Gaiman, Robert E. Howard, and Robert Bloch.

Yet, the fickle finger of fate was not yet done stirring up bitter irony in Lovecraft's troubled life. In the last days before his death, and shortly after he had completed his final short story, *The Haunter of the Dark*, he morosely reflected back to an earlier story he had written—*At the Mountains of Madness*—recalling that it had received such a hostile reception, it "did more than anything to end my effective fictional career." Today, that story is one of Lovecraft's best-known and widely acclaimed tales, and nearly a century later, it regularly bubbles up into the Top Ten bestseller list in classical horror genres.

Chapter 1

I am forced into speech because men of science have refused to follow my advice without knowing why. It is altogether against my will that I tell my reasons for opposing this contemplated invasion of the Antarctic, with its vast fossil hunt and wholesale boring and melting of the ancient ice caps. And I am the more reluctant because my warning may be in vain.

Doubt of the real facts, as I must reveal them, is inevitable; yet, if I suppressed what will seem extravagant and incredible, there would be nothing left. The hitherto withheld photographs, both ordinary and aerial, will count in my favor, for they are damnably vivid and graphic. Still, they will be doubted because of the great lengths to which clever fakery can be carried. The ink drawings, of course, will be jeered as obvious impostures, notwithstanding a strangeness of technique which art experts ought to remark and puzzle over.

In the end, I must rely on the judgment and standing of the few scientific leaders who have, on the one hand, sufficient independence of thought to weigh my data on its own hideously convincing merits or in the light of certain primordial and highly baffling myth-cycles; and on the other hand, sufficient influence to deter the exploring world in general from any rash and over-ambitious program in the region of those mountains of madness. It is an unfortunate fact that relatively obscure men like myself and my associates, connected only with a small university, have little chance of making an impression where matters of a wildly bizarre or highly controversial nature are concerned.

It is further against us that we are not, in the strictest sense, specialists in the fields which came primarily to be concerned. As a geologist, my object in leading the Miskatonic University Expedition was wholly that of securing deep-level specimens of rock and soil from various parts of the Antarctic continent, aided by the remarkable drill devised by Professor Frank H. Pabodie of our engineering department. I had no wish to be a pioneer in any other field than this, but I did hope that the use of this new mechanical appliance at different points along previously explored paths would bring to light materials of a sort hitherto unreached by the ordinary methods of collection.

Pabodie's drilling apparatus, as the public already knows from our reports, was unique and radical in its lightness, portability, and capacity to combine the ordinary artesian drill principle with the principle of the small circular rock drill in such a way as to cope quickly with strata of varying hardness. Steel head, jointed rods, gasoline motor, collapsible wooden derrick, dynamiting paraphernalia, cording, debris-removal auger, and sectional piping for bores five inches wide and up to one thousand feet deep all formed, with needed accessories, no greater load than three seven-dog sledges could carry. This was made possible by the clever aluminum alloy of which most of the metal objects were fashioned. Four large Dornier aeroplanes, designed especially for the tremendous altitude flying necessary on the Antarctic plateau and with added fuel-warming and quick-starting devices worked out by Pabodie, could transport our entire expedition from a base at the edge of the great ice barrier to various suitable inland points, and from these points a sufficient quota of dogs would serve us.

We planned to cover as great an area as one Antarctic season—or longer, if absolutely necessary—would permit, operating mostly in the mountain ranges and on the plateau south of Ross Sea; regions explored in varying degree by Shackleton, Amundsen, Scott, and Byrd. With frequent changes of camp, made by aeroplane and involving distances great enough to be of geological significance, we expected to unearth a quite unprecedented amount of material—especially in the pre-Cambrian strata of which so narrow a range of Antarctic specimens had previously been secured. We wished also to obtain as great as possible a variety of the upper fossiliferous rocks, since the primal life history of this bleak realm of ice and death is of the highest importance to our knowledge of the earth's past. That the Antarctic continent was once temperate and even tropical, with a teeming vegetable and animal life of which the lichens, marine fauna, arachnida, and penguins of the northern edge are the only survivals, is a matter of common information; and we hoped to expand that information in variety, accuracy, and detail. When a simple boring revealed fossiliferous signs, we would enlarge the aperture by blasting to get specimens of suitable size and condition.

Our borings, of varying depth according to the promise held out by the upper soil or rock, were to be confined to exposed, or nearly exposed, land surfaces—these inevitably being slopes and ridges because of the mile or two-mile thickness of solid ice overlying the lower levels. We could not afford to waste drilling the depth of any considerable amount of mere glaciation, though Pabodie had worked out a plan for sinking copper electrodes in thick clusters of borings and melting off limited areas of ice with current from a gasoline-driven dynamo. It is this plan, which we could not put into effect except experimentally on an expedition such as ours, that the coming Starkweather-Moore Expedition proposes to follow, despite the warnings I have issued since our return from the Antarctic.

The public knows of the Miskatonic expedition through our frequent wireless reports to the *Arkham Advertiser* and Associated Press, and through the later articles of Pabodie and myself. We consisted of four men from the University: Pabodie, Lake of the biology department, Atwood of the physics department—also a meteorologist—and myself, representing geology and having nominal command, plus sixteen assistants: seven graduate students from Miskatonic and nine skilled mechanics. Of these sixteen, twelve were qualified aeroplane pilots, all but two of whom were competent wireless operators. Eight of them understood navigation with compass and sextant, as did Pabodie, Atwood, and I. In addition, of course, our two ships—wooden ex-whalers, reinforced for ice conditions and having auxiliary steam—were fully manned.

The Nathaniel Derby Pickman Foundation, aided by a few special contributions, financed the expedition; hence our preparations were extremely thorough, despite the absence of great publicity. The dogs, sledges, machines, camp materials, and unassembled parts of our five planes were delivered in Boston, and there our ships were loaded. We were marvelously well-equipped for our specific purposes, and in all matters pertaining to supplies, regimen, transportation, and camp construction we profited by the excellent example of our many recent and exceptionally brilliant predecessors. It was the unusual number and fame of these predecessors which made our own expedition, ample though it was, so little noticed by the world at large.

As the newspapers told, we sailed from Boston Harbor on September 2nd, 1930, taking a leisurely course down the coast and through the Panama Canal, stopping at Samoa and Hobart, Tasmania, at which latter place we took on final supplies. None of our exploring party had ever been in the polar regions before, hence we all relied greatly on our ship captains, J. B. Douglas, commanding the brig *Arkham*, and serving as commander of the sea party, and Georg Thorfinnssen, commanding the barque *Miskatonic*, both veteran whalers in Antarctic waters.

As we left the inhabited world behind, the sun sank lower and lower in the north, and stayed longer and longer above the horizon each day. At about 62° South Latitude we sighted our first icebergs—table-like objects with vertical sides—and just before reaching the Antarctic circle, which we crossed on October 20th with appropriately quaint ceremonies, we were considerably troubled with field ice. The falling temperature bothered me considerably after our long voyage through the tropics, but I tried to brace up for the worse rigors to come. On many occasions, the curious atmospheric effects enchanted me vastly; these including a strikingly vivid mirage—the first I had ever seen—in which distant bergs became the battlements of unimaginable cosmic castles.

Pushing through the ice, which was fortunately neither extensive nor thickly packed, we regained open water at South Latitude 67°, East Longitude 175° On the morning of October 26th, a strong land blink appeared on the south, and before noon, we all felt a thrill of excitement at beholding a vast, lofty, and snow-clad mountain chain that opened out and covered the whole vista ahead. At last we had encountered an outpost of the great unknown continent and its cryptic world of frozen death. These peaks were obviously the Admiralty Range discovered by Ross, and it would now be our task to round Cape Adare and sail down the east coast of Victoria Land to our contemplated base on the shore of McMurdo Sound, at the foot of the volcano Erebus in South Latitude 77° 9'.

The last lap of the voyage was vivid and fancy-stirring. Great, barren peaks of mystery loomed up constantly against the west as the low northern sun of noon or the still lower horizon-grazing southern sun of midnight poured its hazy reddish rays over the white snow, bluish ice and water lanes, and black bits of exposed granite slope. Through the desolate summits swept raging, intermittent gusts of the terrible Antarctic wind, whose cadences sometimes held vague suggestions of a wild and half-sentient musical piping, with notes extending over a wide range, and which for some subconscious mnemonic reason seemed to me disquieting and even dimly terrible. Something about the scene reminded me of the strange and disturbing Asian paintings of Nicholas Roerich and of the still stranger and more disturbing descriptions of the evilly fabled plateau of Leng that occur in the dreaded *Necronomicon* of the mad Arab Abdul Alhazred. I was rather sorry, later on, that I had ever looked into that monstrous book at the college library.

On November 7th, sight of the westward range having been temporarily lost, we passed Franklin Island; and the next day descried the cones of Mts. Erebus and Terror on Ross Island ahead, with the long line of the Parry Mountains beyond. There now stretched off to the east the low, white line of the great ice barrier, rising perpendicularly to a height of two hundred feet like the rocky cliffs of Quebec, and marking the end of southward navigation. In the afternoon, we entered McMurdo Sound and stood off the coast in the lee of smoking Mt. Erebus. The scoriac peak towered up some twelve thousand, seven hundred feet against the eastern sky, like a Japanese print of the sacred Fujiyama, while beyond it rose the white, ghost-like height of Mt. Terror, ten thousand, nine hundred feet in altitude, and now extinct as a volcano.

Puffs of smoke from Erebus came intermittently, and one of the graduate assistants—a brilliant young fellow named Danforth—pointed out what looked like lava on the snowy slope, remarking that this mountain, discovered in 1840, had undoubtedly been the source of Poe's image when he wrote seven years later:

"—the lavas that restlessly roll
Their sulphurous currents down Yaanek
In the ultimate climes of the pole—
That groan as they roll down Mount Yaanek
In the realms of the boreal pole."

Danforth was a great reader of bizarre material and had talked a good deal of Poe. I was interested myself because of the Antarctic scene of Poe's only long story—the disturbing and enigmatical *Arthur Gordon Pym.* On the barren shore, and on the lofty ice barrier in the background, myriads of animated penguins squawked and flapped their fins, while many fat seals were visible on the water, swimming or sprawling across large cakes of slowly drifting ice.

Using small boats, we effected a difficult landing on Ross Island shortly after midnight on the morning of the 9th, carrying a line of cable from each of the ships and preparing to unload supplies by means of a breeches-buoy arrangement. Our sensations on first treading Antarctic soil were poignant and complex, even though at this particular point, the Scott and Shackleton expeditions had preceded us. Our camp on the frozen shore below the volcano's slope was only a provisional one, headquarters being kept aboard the *Arkham.* We landed all our drilling apparatus, dogs, sledges, tents, provisions, gasoline tanks, experimental ice-melting outfit, cameras, both ordinary and aerial, aeroplane parts, and other accessories, including three small portable wireless outfits—besides those in the planes—capable of communicating with the *Arkham's* large outfit from any part of the Antarctic continent that we would be likely to visit. The ship's outfit, communicating with the outside world, was to convey press reports to the *Arkham Advertiser's* powerful wireless station on Kingsport Head, Massachusetts. We hoped to complete our work during a single Antarctic summer; but if this proved impossible, we would winter on the *Arkham,* sending the *Miskatonic* north before the freezing of the ice for another summer's supplies.

I need not repeat what the newspapers have already published about our early work: of our ascent of Mt. Erebus; our successful mineral borings at several points on Ross Island, and the singular speed with which Pabodie's apparatus accomplished them, even through solid rock layers; our provisional test of the small ice-melting equipment; our perilous ascent of the great barrier with sledges and supplies; and our final assembling of five huge aeroplanes at the camp atop the barrier. The health of our land party—twenty men and fifty-five Alaskan sledge dogs—was remarkable, though of course we had so far encountered no really destructive temperatures or windstorms. For the most part, the thermometer varied between zero and 20° or 25° above, and our experience with New England winters had accustomed us to rigors of this sort. The barrier camp was semi-permanent and destined to be a storage cache for gasoline, provisions, dynamite, and other supplies. Only four of our planes were needed to carry the actual exploring material, the fifth being left with a pilot and two men from the ships at the storage cache to form a means of reaching us from the *Arkham* in case all our exploring planes were lost. Later, when not using all the other planes for moving apparatus, we would employ one or two in a shuttle transportation service between this cache and another permanent base on the great plateau from six hundred to seven hundred miles southward, beyond Beardmore Glacier. Despite the almost unanimous accounts of appalling winds and tempests that pour down from the plateau, we determined to dispense with intermediate bases, taking our chances in the interest of economy and probable efficiency.

Wireless reports have spoken of the breathtaking, four-hour, nonstop flight of our squadron on November 21st over the lofty shelf ice, with vast peaks rising on the west, and the unfathomed silences echoing to the sound of our engines. Wind troubled us only moderately, and our radio compasses helped us through the one opaque fog we encountered. When the vast rise loomed ahead, between latitudes 83° and 84°, we knew we had reached Beardmore Glacier, the largest valley glacier in the world, and that the frozen sea was now giving place to a frowning and mountainous coast line. At last we were truly entering the white, aeon-dead world of the ultimate south. Even as we realized it, we saw the peak of Mt. Nansen in the eastern distance, towering up to its height of almost fifteen thousand feet.

The successful establishment of the southern base above the glacier in latitude 86° 7', east longitude 174° 23', and the phenomenally rapid and effective borings and blastings made at various points reached by our sledge trips and short aeroplane flights, are matters of history; as is the arduous and triumphant ascent of Mt. Nansen by Pabodie and two of the graduate students—Gedney and Carroll—on December 13-15. We were some eight thousand, five hundred feet above sea-level, and when experimental drillings revealed solid ground only twelve feet down through the snow and ice at certain points, we made considerable use of the small melting apparatus and sunk bores and performed dynamiting at many places where no previous explorer had ever thought of securing mineral specimens. The pre-Cambrian granites and beacon sandstones thus obtained confirmed our belief that this plateau was homogeneous, with the great bulk of the continent to the west, but somewhat different from the parts lying eastward below South America—which we then thought to form a separate and smaller continent divided from the larger one by a frozen junction of Ross and Weddell Seas, though Byrd has since disproved the hypothesis.

In certain of the sandstones, dynamited and chiseled after boring revealed their nature, we found some highly interesting fossil markings and fragments; notably ferns, seaweeds, trilobites, crinoids, and such mollusks as linguellae and gastropods—all of which seemed of real significance in connection with the region's primordial history. There was also a queer triangular, striated marking, about a foot in greatest diameter, which Lake pieced together from three fragments of slate brought up from a deep-blasted aperture. These fragments came from a point to the westward, near the Queen Alexandra Range; and Lake, as a biologist, seemed to find their curious marking unusually puzzling and provocative, though to my geological eye it looked not unlike some of the ripple effects reasonably common in the sedimentary rocks. Since slate is no more than a metamorphic formation into which a sedimentary stratum is pressed, and since the pressure itself produces odd distorting effects on any markings which may exist, I saw no reason for extreme wonder over the striated depression.

On January 6th, 1931, Lake, Pabodie, Danforth, the other six students, and myself flew directly over the south pole in two of the great planes, being forced down once by a sudden high wind, which, fortunately, did not develop into a typical storm. This was, as the papers have stated, one of several observation flights, during others of which we tried to discern new topographical features in areas unreached by previous explorers. Our early flights were disappointing in this latter respect, though they afforded us some magnificent examples of the richly fantastic and deceptive mirages of the polar regions, of which our sea voyage had given us some brief foretastes. Distant mountains floated in the sky as enchanted cities, and often the whole white world would dissolve into a gold, silver, and scarlet land of Dunsanian dreams and adventurous expectancy under the magic of the low midnight sun. On cloudy days, we had considerable trouble in flying owing to the tendency of snowy earth and sky to merge into one mystical opalescent void with no visible horizon to mark the junction of the two.

At length we resolved to carry out our original plan of flying five hundred miles eastward with all four exploring planes and establishing a fresh sub-base at a point which would probably be on the smaller continental division, as we mistakenly conceived it. Geological specimens obtained there would be desirable for purposes of comparison. Our health so far had remained excellent—lime juice well offsetting the steady diet of tinned and salted food, and temperatures generally above zero enabling us to do without our thickest furs. It was now midsummer, and with haste and care, we might be able to conclude work by March and avoid a tedious wintering through the long Antarctic night. Several savage windstorms had burst upon us from the west, but we had escaped damage through the skill of Atwood in devising rudimentary aeroplane shelters and windbreaks of heavy snow blocks, and reinforcing the principal camp buildings with snow. Our good luck and efficiency had indeed been almost uncanny.

The outside world knew, of course, of our program, and was told also of Lake's strange and dogged insistence on a westward—or rather, northwestward—prospecting trip before our radical shift to the new base. It seems that he had pondered a great deal, and with alarmingly radical daring, over that triangular striated marking in the slate; reading into it certain contradictions in nature and geological period which whetted his curiosity to the utmost and made him avid to sink more borings and blastings in the west-stretching formation to which the exhumed fragments evidently belonged. He was strangely convinced that the marking was the print of some bulky, unknown, and radically unclassifiable organism of considerably advanced evolution, notwithstanding that the rock which bore it was of so vastly ancient a date—Cambrian if not actually pre-Cambrian—as to preclude the probable existence not only of all highly evolved life, but of any life at all above the unicellular or at most the trilobite stage. These fragments, with their odd marking, must have been five hundred million to a thousand million years old.

Chapter 2

Popular imagination, I judge, responded actively to our wireless bulletins of Lake's start northwestward into regions never trodden by human foot or penetrated by human imagination, though we did not mention his wild hopes of revolutionizing the entire sciences of biology and geology. His preliminary sledging and boring journey of January 11th to 18th with Pabodie and five others—marred by the loss of two dogs in an upset when crossing one of the great pressure ridges in the ice—had brought up more and more of the Archaean slate; and even I was interested by the singular profusion of evident fossil markings in that unbelievably ancient stratum. These markings, however, were of very primitive life forms involving no great paradox except that any life forms should occur in rock as definitely pre-Cambrian as this seemed to be; hence, I still failed to see the good sense of Lake's demand for an interlude in our time-saving program—an interlude requiring the use of all four planes, many men, and the whole of the expedition's mechanical apparatus. I did not, in the end, veto the plan, though I decided not to accompany the northwestward party despite Lake's plea for my geological advice. While they were gone, I would remain at the base with Pabodie and five men and work out final plans for the eastward shift. In preparation for this transfer, one of the planes had begun to move up a good gasoline supply from McMurdo Sound; but this could wait temporarily. I kept with me one sledge and nine dogs, since it is unwise to be at any time without possible transportation in an utterly tenantless world of aeon-long death.

Lake's sub-expedition into the unknown, as everyone will recall, sent out its own reports from the shortwave transmitters on the planes; these being simultaneously picked up by our apparatus at the southern base and by the *Arkham* at McMurdo Sound, whence they were relayed to the outside world on wavelengths up to fifty meters. The start was made January 22nd at 4 a.m., and the first wireless message we received came only two hours later, when Lake spoke of descending and starting a small-scale ice-melting and bore at a point some three hundred miles away from us. Six hours after that, a second and very excited message told of the frantic, beaver-like work whereby a shallow shaft had been sunk and blasted, culminating in the discovery of slate fragments with several markings approximately like the one which had caused the original puzzlement.

Three hours later, a brief bulletin announced the resumption of the flight in the teeth of a raw and piercing gale; and when I dispatched a message of protest against further hazards, Lake replied curtly that his new specimens made any hazard worth taking. I saw that his excitement had reached the point of mutiny, and that I could do nothing to check this headlong risk of the whole expedition's success; but it was appalling to think of his plunging deeper and deeper into that treacherous and sinister white immensity of tempests and unfathomed mysteries which stretched off for some fifteen hundred miles to the half-known, half-suspected coast line of Queen Mary and Knox Lands.

Then, in about an hour and a half more, came that doubly excited message from Lake's moving plane, which almost reversed my sentiments and made me wish I had accompanied the party:

> "10:05 p.m. On the wing. After snowstorm, have spied mountain range ahead higher than any hitherto seen. May equal Himalayas, allowing for height of plateau. Probable Latitude 76° 15', Longitude 113° 10' E. Reaches far as can see to right and left. Suspicion of two smoking cones. All peaks black and bare of snow. Gale blowing off them impedes navigation."

After that Pabodie, the men, and I hung breathlessly over the receiver. Thought of this titanic mountain rampart seven hundred miles away inflamed our deepest sense of adventure; and we rejoiced that our expedition, if not ourselves personally, had been its discoverers. In half an hour, Lake called us again:

> "Moulton's plane forced down on plateau in foothills, but nobody hurt and perhaps can repair. Shall transfer essentials to other three for return or further moves if necessary, but no more heavy plane travel needed just now. Mountains surpass anything in imagination. Am going up scouting in Carroll's plane, with all weight out. You can't imagine anything like this. Highest peaks must go over thirty-five thousand feet. Everest out of the running. Atwood to work out height with theodolite while Carroll and I go up. Probably wrong about cones, for formations look stratified. Possibly pre-Cambrian slate with other strata mixed in. Queer skyline effects—regular sections of cubes clinging to highest peaks. Whole thing marvelous in red-gold light of low sun. Like land of mystery in a dream or gateway to forbidden world of untrodden wonder. Wish you were here to study."

Though it was technically sleeping-time, not one of us listeners thought for a moment of retiring. It must have been a good deal the same at McMurdo Sound, where the supply cache and the *Arkham* LAO were getting the messages; for Captain Douglas gave out a call congratulating everybody on the important find, and Sherman, the cache operator, seconded his sentiments. We were sorry, of course, about the damaged aeroplane, but hoped it could be easily mended. Then, at 11 P.M., came another call from Lake:

> "Up with Carroll over highest foothills. Don't dare try really tall peaks in present weather, but shall later. Frightful work climbing, and hard going at this altitude, but worth it. Great range fairly solid, hence can't get any glimpses beyond. Main summits exceed Himalayas, and very queer. Range looks like pre-Cambrian slate, with plain signs of many other upheaved strata. Was wrong about volcanism. Goes farther in either direction than we can see. Swept clear of snow above about twenty-one thousand feet. Odd formations on slopes of highest mountains. Great low square blocks with exactly vertical sides, and rectangular lines of low, vertical ramparts, like the old Asian castles clinging to steep mountains in Roerich's paintings. Impressive from distance. Flew close to some, and Carroll thought they were formed of smaller separate pieces, but that is probably weathering. Most edges crumbled and rounded off as if exposed to storms and climate changes for millions of years. Parts, especially upper parts, seem to be of lighter-colored rock than any visible strata on slopes proper, hence of evidently crystalline origin. Close flying shows many cave-mouths, some unusually regular in outline, square or semicircular. You must come and investigate. Think I saw rampart squarely on top of one peak. Height seems about thirty thousand to thirty-five thousand feet. Am up twenty-one thousand, five hundred myself, in devilish, gnawing cold. Wind whistles and pipes through passes and in and out of caves, but no flying danger so far."

From then on for another half hour, Lake kept up a running fire of comment, and expressed his intention of climbing some of the peaks on foot. I replied that I would join him as soon as he could send a plane, and that Pabodie and I would work out the best gasoline plan—just where and how to concentrate our supply in view of the expedition's altered character. Obviously, Lake's boring operations, as well as his aeroplane activities, would require a great deal for the new base that he planned to establish at the foot of the mountains; and it was possible that the eastward flight might not be made, after all, this season. In connection with this business, I called Captain Douglas and asked him to get as much as possible out of the ships and up the barrier with the single dog team we had left there. A direct route across the unknown region between Lake and McMurdo Sound was what we really ought to establish.

Lake called me later to say that he had decided to let the camp stay where Moulton's plane had been forced down, and where repairs had already progressed somewhat. The ice sheet was very thin, with dark ground here and there visible, and he would sink some borings and blasts at that very point before making any sledge trips or climbing expeditions. He spoke of the ineffable majesty of the whole scene, and the queer state of his sensations at being in the lee of vast, silent pinnacles whose ranks shot up like a wall reaching the sky at the world's rim. Atwood's theodolite observations had placed the height of the five tallest peaks at from thirty thousand to thirty-four thousand feet. The windswept nature of the terrain clearly disturbed Lake, for it argued the occasional existence of prodigious gales, violent beyond anything we had so far encountered. His camp lay a little more than five miles from where the higher foothills rose abruptly. I could almost trace a note of subconscious alarm in his words—flashed across a glacial void of seven hundred miles—as he urged that we all hasten with the matter and get the strange, new region disposed of as soon as possible. He was about to rest now, after a continuous day's work of almost unparalleled speed, strenuousness, and results.

In the morning, I had a three-cornered wireless talk with Lake and Captain Douglas at their widely separated bases. It was agreed that one of Lake's planes would come to my base for Pabodie, the five men, and myself, as well as for all the fuel it could carry. The rest of the fuel question, depending on our decision about an easterly trip, could wait for a few days, since Lake had enough for immediate camp heat and borings. Eventually the old southern base ought to be restocked, but if we postponed the easterly trip, we would not use it till the next summer, and, meanwhile, Lake must send a plane to explore a direct route between his new mountains and McMurdo Sound.

Pabodie and I prepared to close our base for a short or long period, as the case might be. If we wintered in the Antarctic, we would probably fly straight from Lake's base to the *Arkham* without returning to this spot. Some of our conical tents had already been reinforced by blocks of hard snow, and now we decided to complete the job of making a permanent village. Owing to a very liberal tent supply, Lake had with him all that his base would need, even after our arrival. I wirelessed that Pabodie and I would be ready for the northwestward move after one day's work and one night's rest.

Our labors, however, were not very steady after 4 p.m., for about that time, Lake began sending in the most extraordinary and excited messages. His working day had started unpropitiously, since an aeroplane survey of the nearly-exposed rock surfaces showed an entire absence of those Archaean and primordial strata for which he was looking, and which formed so great a part of the colossal peaks that loomed up at a tantalizing distance from the camp. Most of the rocks glimpsed were apparently Jurassic and Comanchian sandstones and Permian and Triassic schists, with now and then a glossy black outcropping suggesting a hard and slaty coal. This discouraged Lake, whose plans all hinged on unearthing specimens more than five hundred million years older. It was clear to him that in order to recover the Archaean slate vein in which he had found the odd markings, he would have to make a long sledge trip from these foothills to the steep slopes of the gigantic mountains themselves.

He had resolved, nevertheless, to do some local boring as part of the expedition's general program; hence, he set up the drill and put five men to work with it while the rest finished settling the camp and repairing the damaged aeroplane. The softest visible rock—a sandstone about a quarter of a mile from the camp—had been chosen for the first sampling; and the drill made excellent progress without much supplementary blasting. It was about three hours afterward, following the first really heavy blast of the operation, that the shouting of the drill crew was heard; and that young Gedney—the acting foreman—rushed into the camp with the startling news.

They had struck a cave. Early in the boring, the sandstone had given place to a vein of Comanchian limestone, full of minute fossil cephalonpods, corals, echini, and spirifera, and with occasional suggestions of siliceous sponges and marine vertebrate bones—the latter probably of teleosts, sharks, and ganoids. This, in itself, was important enough, as affording the first vertebrate fossils the expedition had yet secured; but when shortly afterward the drill head dropped through the stratum into apparent vacancy, a wholly new and doubly intense wave of excitement spread among the excavators. A good-sized blast had laid open the subterrene secret; and now, through a jagged aperture perhaps five feet across and three feet thick, there yawned before the avid searchers a section of shallow limestone hollowing worn more than fifty million years ago by the trickling ground waters of a bygone tropic world.

The hollowed layer was not more than seven or eight feet deep but extended off indefinitely in all directions and had a fresh, slightly moving air which suggested its membership in an extensive subterranean system. Its roof and floor were abundantly equipped with large stalactites and stalagmites, some of which met in columnar form: but important above all else was the vast deposit of shells and bones, which in places nearly choked the passage. Washed down from unknown jungles of Mesozoic tree ferns and fungi, and forests of Tertiary cycads, fan palms, and primitive angiosperms, this osseous medley contained representatives of more Cretaceous, Eocene, and other animal species than the greatest paleontologist could have counted or classified in a year. Mollusks, crustacean armor, fishes, amphibians, reptiles, birds, and early mammals—great and small, known and unknown. No wonder Gedney ran back to the camp shouting, and no wonder everyone else dropped work and rushed headlong through the biting cold to where the tall derrick marked a newfound gateway to secrets of inner earth and vanished aeons.

When Lake had satisfied the first keen edge of his curiosity, he scribbled a message in his notebook and had young Moulton run back to the camp to dispatch it by wireless. This was my first word of the discovery, and it told of the identification of early shells, bones of ganoids and placoderms, remnants of labyrinthodonts and thecodonts, great mosasaur skull fragments, dinosaur vertebrae and armor plates, pterodactyl teeth and wing bones, Archaeopteryx debris, Miocene sharks' teeth, primitive bird skulls, and other bones of archaic mammals such as palaeotheres, Xiphodons, Eohippi, Oreodons, and titanotheres. There was nothing as recent as a mastodon, elephant, true camel, deer, or bovine animal; hence Lake concluded that the last deposits had occurred during the Oligocene Age, and that the hollowed stratum had lain in its present dried, dead, and inaccessible state for at least thirty million years.

On the other hand, the prevalence of very early life forms was singular in the highest degree. Though the limestone formation was, on the evidence of such typical imbedded fossils as ventriculites, positively and unmistakably Comanchian and not a particle earlier, the free fragments in the hollow space included a surprising proportion from organisms hitherto considered as peculiar to far older periods—even rudimentary fishes, mollusks, and corals as remote as the Silurian or Ordovician. The inevitable inference was that in this part of the world there had been a remarkable and unique degree of continuity between the life of over three hundred million years ago and that of only thirty million years ago. How far this continuity had extended beyond the Oligocene Age when the cavern was closed was of course past all speculation. In any event, the coming of the frightful ice in the Pleistocene some five hundred thousand years ago—a mere yesterday as compared with the age of this cavity—must have put an end to any of the primal forms which had locally managed to outlive their common terms.

Lake was not content to let his first message stand, but had another bulletin written and dispatched across the snow to the camp before Moulton could get back. After that, Moulton stayed at the wireless in one of the planes, transmitting to me—and to the *Arkham* for relaying to the outside world—the frequent postscripts which Lake sent him by a succession of messengers. Those who followed the newspapers will remember the excitement created among men of science by that afternoon's reports—reports which have finally led, after all these years, to the organization of that very Starkweather-Moore Expedition which I am so anxious to dissuade from its purposes. I had better give the messages literally as Lake sent them, and as our base operator McTighe translated them from the pencil shorthand:

"Fowler makes discovery of highest importance in sandstone and limestone fragments from blasts. Several distinct triangular striated prints like those in Archaean slate, proving that source survived from over six hundred million years ago to Comanchian times without more than moderate morphological changes and decrease in average size. Comanchian prints apparently more primitive or decadent, if anything, than older ones. Emphasize importance of discovery in press. Will mean to biology what Einstein has meant to mathematics and physics. Joins up with my previous work and amplifies conclusions. Appears to indicate, as I suspected, that earth has seen whole cycle or cycles of organic life before known one that begins with Archaeozoic cells. Was evolved and specialized not later than a thousand million years ago, when planet was young and recently uninhabitable for any life forms or normal protoplasmic structure. Question arises when, where, and how development took place."

"Later. Examining certain skeletal fragments of large land and marine saurians and primitive mammals, find singular local wounds or injuries to bony structure not attributable to any known predatory or carnivorous animal of any period, of two sorts—straight, penetrant bores, and apparently hacking incisions. One or two cases of cleanly severed bones. Not many specimens affected. Am sending to camp for electric torches. Will extend search area underground by hacking away stalactites."

"Still later. Have found peculiar soapstone fragment about six inches across and an inch and a half thick, wholly unlike any visible local formation—greenish, but no evidence to place its period. Has curious smoothness and regularity. Shaped like five-pointed star with tips broken off, and signs of other cleavage at inward angles and in center of surface. Small, smooth depression in center of unbroken surface. Arouses much curiosity as to source and weathering. Probably some freak of water action. Carroll, with magnifier, thinks he can make out additional markings of geologic significance. Groups of tiny dots in regular patterns. Dogs growing uneasy as we work, and seem to hate this soapstone. Must see if it has any peculiar odor. Will report again when Mills gets back with light and we start on underground area."

"10:15 p.m. Important discovery. Orrendorf and Watkins, working underground at 9:45 with light, found monstrous barrel-shaped fossil of wholly unknown nature; probably vegetable unless overgrown specimen of unknown marine radiata. Tissue evidently preserved by mineral salts. Tough as leather, but astonishing flexibility retained in places. Marks of broken-off parts at ends and around sides. Six feet end to end, three and five-tenths feet central diameter, tapering to one foot at each end. Like a barrel with five bulging ridges in place of staves. Lateral breakages, as of thinnish stalks, are at equator in middle of these ridges. In furrows between ridges are curious growths—combs or wings that fold up and spread out like fans. All greatly damaged but one, which gives almost seven-foot wing spread. Arrangement reminds one of certain monsters of primal myth, especially fabled Elder Things in *Necronomicon.* These wings seem to be membranous, stretched on frame work of glandular tubing. Apparent minute orifices in frame tubing at wing tips. Ends of body shriveled, giving no clue to interior or to what has been broken off there. Must dissect when we get back to camp. Can't decide whether vegetable or animal. Many features obviously of almost incredible primitiveness. Have set all hands cutting stalactites and looking for further specimens. More scarred bones found, but these must wait. Having trouble with dogs. They can't endure the new specimen, and would probably tear it to pieces if we didn't keep it at a distance from them."

"11:30 p.m. Attention, Dyer, Pabodie, Douglas. Matter of highest—I might say transcendent—importance. *Arkham* must relay to Kingsport Head Station at once. Strange barrel growth is the Archaean thing that left prints in rocks. Mills, Boudreau, and Fowler discover cluster of thirteen more at underground point forty feet from aperture. Mixed with curiously rounded and configured soapstone fragments smaller than one previously found—star-shaped, but no marks of breakage except at some of the points. Of organic specimens, eight apparently perfect, with all appendages. Have brought all to surface, leading off dogs to distance. They cannot stand the things. Give close attention to description and repeat back for accuracy Papers must get this right.

"Objects are eight feet long all over. Six-foot, five-ridged barrel torso three and five-tenths feet central diameter, one-foot end diameters. Dark gray, flexible, and infinitely tough. Seven-foot membranous wings of same color, found folded, spread out of furrows between ridges. Wing framework tubular or glandular, of lighter gray, with orifices at wing tips. Spread wings have serrated edge. Around equator, one at central apex of each of the five vertical, stave-like ridges are five systems of light gray flexible arms or tentacles found tightly folded to torso but expansible to maximum length of over three feet. Like arms of primitive crinoid. Single stalks three inches diameter branch after six inches into five sub-stalks, each of which branches after eight inches into small, tapering tentacles or tendrils, giving each stalk a total of twenty-five tentacles.

"At top of torso blunt, bulbous neck of lighter gray, with gill-like suggestions, holds yellowish five-pointed starfish-shaped apparent head covered with three-inch wiry cilia of various prismatic colors. Head thick and puffy, about two feet point to point, with three-inch flexible yellowish tubes projecting from each point. Slit in exact center of top probably breathing aperture. At end of each tube is spherical expansion where yellowish membrane rolls back on handling to reveal glassy, red-irised globe, evidently an eye. Five slightly longer reddish tubes start from inner angles of starfish-shaped head and end in saclike swellings of same color which, upon pressure, open to bell-shaped orifices two inches maximum diameter and lined with sharp, white tooth like projections—probably mouths. All these tubes, cilia, and points of starfish head, found folded tightly down; tubes and points clinging to bulbous neck and torso. Flexibility surprising despite vast toughness.

"At bottom of torso, rough but dissimilarly functioning counterparts of head arrangements exist. Bulbous light-gray pseudo-neck, without gill suggestions, holds greenish five-pointed starfish arrangement. Tough, muscular arms four feet long and tapering from seven inches diameter at base to about two and five-tenths at point. To each point is attached small end of a greenish five-veined membranous triangle eight inches long and six wide at farther end. This is the paddle, fin, or pseudo-foot which has made prints in rocks from a thousand million to fifty or sixty million years old. From inner angles of starfish-arrangement project two-foot reddish tubes tapering from three inches diameter at base to one at tip. Orifices at tips. All these parts infinitely tough and leathery, but extremely flexible. Four-foot arms with paddles undoubtedly used for locomotion of some sort, marine or otherwise. When moved, display suggestions of exaggerated muscularity. As found, all these projections tightly folded over pseudo-neck and end of torso, corresponding to projections at other end.

"Cannot yet assign positively to animal or vegetable kingdom, but odds now favor animal. Probably represents incredibly advanced evolution of radiata without loss of certain primitive features. Echinoderm resemblances unmistakable despite local contradictory evidences. Wing structure puzzles in view of probable marine habitat, but may have use in water navigation. Symmetry is curiously vegetable-like, suggesting vegetable's essential up-and-down structure rather than animal's fore-and-aft structure. Fabulously early date of evolution, preceding even simplest Archaean protozoa hitherto known, baffles all conjecture as to origin.

"Complete specimens have such uncanny resemblance to certain creatures of primal myth that suggestion of ancient existence outside Antarctic becomes inevitable. Dyer and Pabodie have read *Necronomican* and seen Clark Ashton Smith's nightmare paintings based on text, and will understand when I speak of Elder Things supposed to have created all earth life as jest or mistake. Students have always thought conception formed from morbid imaginative treatment of very ancient tropical radiata. Also like prehistoric folklore things Wilmarth has spoken of—Cthulhu cult appendages, etc.

"Vast field of study opened. Deposits probably of late Cretaceous or early Eocene period, judging from associated specimens. Massive stalagmites deposited above them. Hard work hewing out, but toughness prevented damage. State of preservation miraculous, evidently owing to limestone action. No more found so far, but will resume search later. Job now to get fourteen huge specimens to camp without dogs, which bark furiously and can't be trusted near them. With nine men—three left to guard the dogs—we ought to manage the three sledges fairly well, though wind is bad. Must establish plane communication with McMurdo Sound and begin shipping material. But I've got to dissect one of these things before we take any rest. Wish I had a real laboratory here. Dyer better kick himself for having tried to stop my westward trip. First, the world's greatest mountains, and then this. If this last isn't the high spot of the expedition, I don't know what is. We're made scientifically. Congrats, Pabodie, on the drill that opened up the cave. Now will *Arkham* please repeat description?"

The sensations of Pabodie and myself at receipt of this report were almost beyond description, nor were our companions much behind us in enthusiasm. McTighe, who had hastily translated a few high spots as they came from the droning receiving set, wrote out the entire message from his shorthand version as soon as Lake's operator signed off. All appreciated the epoch-making significance of the discovery, and I sent Lake congratulations as soon as the *Arkham's* operator had repeated back the descriptive parts as requested; and my example was followed by Sherman from his station at the McMurdo Sound supply cache, as well as by Captain Douglas of the *Arkham*. Later, as head of the Pabodie Expedition, I added some remarks to be relayed through the *Arkham* to the outside world. Of course, rest was an absurd thought amidst this excitement; and my only wish was to get to Lake's camp as quickly as I could. It disappointed me when he sent word that a rising mountain gale made early aerial travel impossible.

But within an hour and a half interest again rose to banish disappointment. Lake, sending more messages, told of the completely successful transportation of the fourteen great specimens to the camp. It had been a hard pull, for the things were surprisingly heavy; but nine men had accomplished it very neatly. Now some of the party were hurriedly building a snow corral at a safe distance from the camp, to which the dogs could be brought for greater convenience in feeding. The specimens were laid out on the hard snow near the camp, save for one on which Lake was making crude attempts at dissection.

This dissection seemed to be a greater task than had been expected, for, despite the heat of a gasoline stove in the newly raised laboratory tent, the deceptively flexible tissues of the chosen specimen—a powerful and intact one—lost nothing of their more than leathery toughness. Lake was puzzled as to how he might make the requisite incisions without violence destructive enough to upset all the structural niceties he was looking for. He had, it is true, seven more perfect specimens; but these were too few to use up recklessly unless the cave might later yield an unlimited supply. Accordingly, he removed the specimen and dragged in one which, though having remnants of the starfish arrangements at both ends, was badly crushed and partly disrupted along one of the great torso furrows.

Results, quickly reported over the wireless, were baffling and provocative indeed. Nothing like delicacy or accuracy was possible with instruments hardly able to cut the anomalous tissue, but the little that was achieved left us all awed and bewildered. Existing biology would have to be wholly revised, for this thing was no product of any cell growth science knows about. There had been scarcely any mineral replacement, and despite an age of perhaps forty million years, the internal organs were wholly intact. The leathery, undeteriorative, and almost indestructible quality was an inherent attribute of the thing's form of organization and pertained to some paleogean cycle of invertebrate evolution utterly beyond our powers of speculation. At first, all that Lake found was dry, but as the heated tent produced its thawing effect, organic moisture of pungent and offensive odor was encountered toward the thing's uninjured side. It was not blood, but a thick, dark-green fluid apparently answering the same purpose. By the time Lake reached this stage, all thirty-seven dogs had been brought to the still uncompleted corral near the camp, and even at that distance set up a savage barking and show of restlessness at the acrid, diffusive smell.

Far from helping to place the strange entity, this provisional dissection merely deepened its mystery. All guesses about its external members had been correct, and on the evidence of these one could hardly hesitate to call the thing animal; but internal inspection brought up so many vegetable evidences that Lake was left hopelessly at sea. It had digestion and circulation, and eliminated waste matter through the reddish tubes of its starfish-shaped base. Cursorily, one would say that its respiration apparatus handled oxygen rather than carbon dioxide, and there were odd evidences of air-storage chambers and methods of shifting respiration from the external orifice to at least two other fully developed breathing systems—gills and pores. Clearly, it was amphibian, and probably adapted to long airless hibernation periods as well. Vocal organs seemed present in connection with the main respiratory system, but they presented anomalies beyond immediate solution. Articulate speech, in the sense of syllable utterance, seemed barely conceivable, but musical piping notes covering a wide range were highly probable. The muscular system was almost prematurely developed.

The nervous system was so complex and highly developed as to leave Lake aghast. Though excessively primitive and archaic in some respects, the thing had a set of ganglial centers and connectives arguing the very extremes of specialized development. Its five-lobed brain was surprisingly advanced, and there were signs of a sensory equipment, served in part through the wiry cilia of the head, involving factors alien to any other terrestrial organism. Probably it had more than five senses, so that its habits could not be predicted from any existing analogy. It must, Lake thought, have been a creature of keen sensitiveness and delicately differentiated functions in its primal world—much like the ants and bees of today. It reproduced like the vegetable cryptogams, especially the Pteridophyta, having spore cases at the tips of the wings and evidently developing from a thallus or prothallus.

But to give it a name at this stage was mere folly. It looked like a radiate, but was clearly something more. It was partly vegetable, but had three-fourths of the essentials of animal structure. That it was marine in origin, its symmetrical contour and certain other attributes clearly indicated; yet one could not be exact as to the limit of its later adaptations. The wings held a persistent suggestion of the aerial. How it could have undergone its tremendously complex evolution on a new-born earth in time to leave prints in Archaean rocks was so far beyond conception as to make Lake whimsically recall the primal myths about Great Old Ones who filtered down from the stars and concocted earth life as a joke or mistake; and the wild tales of cosmic hill things from outside told by a folklorist colleague in Miskatonic's English department.

Naturally, he considered the possibility of the pre-Cambrian prints having been made by a less evolved ancestor of the present specimens, but quickly rejected this too-facile theory upon considering the advanced structural qualities of the older fossils. If anything, the later contours showed decadence rather than higher evolution. The size of the pseudo-feet had decreased, and the whole morphology seemed coarsened and simplified. Moreover, the nerves and organs just examined held singular suggestions of retrogression from forms still more complex. Atrophied and vestigial parts were surprisingly prevalent. Altogether, little could be said to have been solved; and Lake fell back on mythology for a provisional name—jocosely dubbing his finds "The Elder Ones."

At about 2:30 a.m., having decided to postpone further work and get a little rest, he covered the dissected organism with a tarpaulin, emerged from the laboratory tent, and studied the intact specimens with renewed interest. The ceaseless Antarctic sun had begun to limber up their tissues a trifle, so that the head points and tubes of two or three showed signs of unfolding; but Lake did not believe there was any danger of immediate decomposition in the almost subzero air. He did, however, move all the undissected specimens close together and throw a spare tent over them in order to keep off the direct solar rays. That would also help to keep their possible scent away from the dogs, whose hostile unrest was really becoming a problem, even at their substantial distance and behind the higher and higher snow walls which an increased quota of the men were hastening to raise around their quarters. He had to weight down the corners of the tent cloth with heavy blocks of snow to hold it in place amidst the rising gale, for the titan mountains seemed about to deliver some gravely severe blasts. Early apprehensions about sudden Antarctic winds were revived, and under Atwood's supervision precautions were taken to bank the tents, new dog corral, and crude aeroplane shelters with snow on the mountainward side. These latter shelters, begun with hard snow blocks during odd moments, were by no means as high as they should have been; and Lake finally detached all hands from other tasks to work on them.

It was after four when Lake at last prepared to sign off and advised us all to share the rest period his outfit would take when the shelter walls were a little higher. He held some friendly chat with Pabodie over the ether, and repeated his praise of the really marvelous drills that had helped him make his discovery. Atwood also sent greetings and praises. I gave Lake a warm word of congratulations, owning up that he was right about the western trip, and we all agreed to get in touch by wireless at ten in the morning. If the gale was then over, Lake would send a plane for the party at my base. Just before retiring, I dispatched a final message to the *Arkham* with instructions about toning down the day's news for the outside world, since the full details seemed radical enough to rouse a wave of incredulity until further substantiated.

Chapter 3

None of us, I imagine, slept very heavily or continuously that morning. Both the excitement of Lake's discovery and the mounting fury of the wind were against such a thing. So savage was the blast, even where we were, that we could not help wondering how much worse it was at Lake's camp, directly under the vast unknown peaks that bred and delivered it. McTighe was awake at ten o'clock and tried to get Lake on the wireless, as agreed, but some electrical condition in the disturbed air to the westward seemed to prevent communication. We did, however, get the *Arkham*, and Douglas told me that he had likewise been vainly trying to reach Lake. He had not known about the wind, for very little was blowing at McMurdo Sound, despite its persistent rage where we were.

Throughout the day, we all listened anxiously and tried to get Lake at intervals, but invariably without results. About noon, a positive frenzy of wind stampeded out of the west, causing us to fear for the safety of our camp; but it eventually died down, with only a moderate relapse at 2 p.m. After three o'clock, it was very quiet, and we redoubled our efforts to get Lake. Reflecting that he had four planes, each provided with an excellent shortwave outfit, we could not imagine any ordinary accident capable of crippling all his wireless equipment at once. Nevertheless, the stony silence continued, and when we thought of the delirious force the wind must have had in his locality, we could not help making the most direful conjectures.

By six o'clock, our fears had become intense and definite, and after a wireless consultation with Douglas and Thorfinnssen, I resolved to take steps toward investigation. The fifth aeroplane, which we had left at the McMurdo Sound supply cache with Sherman and two sailors, was in good shape and ready for instant use, and it seemed that the very emergency for which it had been saved was now upon us. I got Sherman by wireless and ordered him to join me with the plane and the two sailors at the southern base as quickly as possible, the air conditions being apparently highly favorable. We then talked over the personnel of the coming investigation party, and decided that we would include all hands, together with the sledge and dogs which I had kept with me. Even so great a load would not be too much for one of the huge planes built to our special orders for heavy machinery transportation. At intervals I still tried to reach Lake with the wireless, but all to no purpose.

Sherman, with the sailors Gunnarsson and Larsen, took off at 7:30, and reported a quiet flight from several points on the wing. They arrived at our base at midnight, and all hands at once discussed the next move. It was risky business sailing over the Antarctic in a single aeroplane without any line of bases, but no one drew back from what seemed like the plainest necessity. We turned in at two o'clock for a brief rest after some preliminary loading of the plane, but were up again in four hours to finish the loading and packing.

At 7:15 a.m., January 25th, we started flying northwestward under McTighe's pilotage with ten men, seven dogs, a sledge, a fuel and food supply, and other items including the plane's wireless outfit. The atmosphere was clear, fairly quiet, and relatively mild in temperature, and we anticipated very little trouble in reaching the latitude and longitude designated by Lake as the site of his camp. Our apprehensions were over what we might find, or fail to find, at the end of our journey, for silence continued to answer all calls dispatched to the camp.

Every incident of that four-and-a-half-hour flight is burned into my recollection because of its crucial position in my life. It marked my loss, at the age of fifty-four, of all that peace and balance which the normal mind possesses through its accustomed conception of external nature and nature's laws. Thenceforward the ten of us—but the student Danforth and myself above all others—were to face a hideously amplified world of lurking horrors which nothing can erase from our emotions, and which we would refrain from sharing with mankind in general if we could. The newspapers have printed the bulletins we sent from the moving plane, telling of our non-stop course, our two battles with treacherous upper-air gales, our glimpse of the broken surface where Lake had sunk his mid-journey shaft three days before, and our sight of a group of those strange, fluffy snow cylinders noted by Amundsen and Byrd as rolling in the wind across the endless leagues of frozen plateau. There came a point, though, when our sensations could not be conveyed in any words the press would understand, and a latter point when we had to adopt an actual rule of strict censorship.

The sailor Larsen was first to spy the jagged line of witch-like cones and pinnacles ahead, and his shouts sent everyone to the windows of the great cabined plane. Despite our speed, they were very slow in gaining prominence; hence we knew that they must be infinitely far off, and visible only because of their abnormal height. Little by little, however, they rose grimly into the western sky; allowing us to distinguish various bare, bleak, blackish summits, and to catch the curious sense of fantasy which they inspired as seen in the reddish Antarctic light against the provocative background of iridescent ice-dust clouds. In the whole spectacle, there was a persistent, pervasive hint of stupendous secrecy and potential revelation. It was as if these stark, nightmare spires marked the pylons of a frightful gateway into forbidden spheres of dream, and complex gulfs of remote time, space, and ultra-dimensionality. I could not help feeling that they were evil things—mountains of madness whose farther slopes looked out over some accursed, ultimate abyss. That seething, half-luminous cloud background held ineffable suggestions of a vague, ethereal *beyondness* far more than terrestrially spatial and gave appalling reminders of the utter remoteness, separateness, desolation, and aeon-long death of this untrodden and unfathomed austral world.

It was young Danforth who drew our notice to the curious regularities of the higher mountain skyline—regularities like clinging fragments of perfect cubes, which Lake had mentioned in his messages, and which indeed justified his comparison with the dreamlike suggestions of primordial temple ruins, on cloudy Asian mountaintops so subtly and strangely painted by Roerich. There was indeed something hauntingly Roerich-like about this whole unearthly continent of mountainous mystery. I had felt it in October when we first caught sight of Victoria Land, and I felt it afresh now. I felt, too, another wave of uneasy consciousness of Archaean mythical resemblances; of how disturbingly this lethal realm corresponded to the evilly famed plateau of Leng in the primal writings. Mythologists have placed Leng in Central Asia; but the racial memory of man—or of his predecessors—is long, and it may well be that certain tales have come down from lands and mountains and temples of horror earlier than Asia and earlier than any human world we know. A few daring mystics have hinted at a pre-Pleistocene origin for the fragmentary Pnakotic Manuscripts, and have suggested that the devotees of Tsathoggua were as alien to mankind as Tsathoggua itself. Leng, wherever in space or time it might brood, was not a region I would care to be in or near, nor did I relish the proximity of a world that had ever bred such ambiguous and Archaean monstrosities as those Lake had just mentioned. At the moment, I felt sorry that I had ever read the abhorred *Necronomicon* or talked so much with that unpleasantly erudite folklorist Wilmarth at the university.

This mood undoubtedly served to aggravate my reaction to the bizarre mirage which burst upon us from the increasingly opalescent zenith as we drew near the mountains and began to make out the cumulative undulations of the foothills. I had seen dozens of polar mirages during the preceding weeks, some of them quite as uncanny and fantastically vivid as the present sample; but this one had a wholly novel and obscure quality of menacing symbolism, and I shuddered as the seething labyrinth of fabulous walls and towers and minarets loomed out of the troubled ice vapors above our heads.

The effect was that of a Cyclopean city of no architecture known to man or to human imagination, with vast aggregations of night-black masonry embodying monstrous perversions of geometrical laws. There were truncated cones, sometimes terraced or fluted, surmounted by tall cylindrical shafts here and there bulbously enlarged and often capped with tiers of thinnish scalloped disks; and strange beetling, table-like constructions suggesting piles of multitudinous rectangular slabs or circular plates or five-pointed stars with each one overlapping the one beneath. There were composite cones and pyramids either alone or surmounting cylinders or cubes or flatter truncated cones and pyramids, and occasional needle-like spires in curious clusters of five. All of these febrile structures seemed knit together by tubular bridges crossing from one to the other at various dizzy heights, and the implied scale of the whole was terrifying and oppressive in its sheer gigantism. The general type of mirage was not unlike some of the wilder forms observed and drawn by the arctic whaler Scoresby in 1820, but at this time and place, with those dark, unknown mountain peaks soaring stupendously ahead, that anomalous elder-world discovery in our minds, and the pall of probable disaster enveloping the greater part of our expedition, we all seemed to find in it a taint of latent malignity and infinitely evil portent.

I was glad when the mirage began to break up, although in the process the various nightmare turrets and cones assumed distorted, temporary forms seemingly even more hideous. As the whole illusion dissolved to churning opalescence, we began to look earthward again, and saw that our journey's end was not far off. The unknown mountains ahead rose dizzily up like a fearsome rampart of giants, their curious regularities showing with startling clearness even without a field-glass. We were over the lowest foothills now, and could see amidst the snow, ice, and bare patches of their main plateau a couple of darkish spots which we took to be Lake's camp and boring. The higher foothills shot up between five and six miles away, forming a range almost distinct from the terrifying line of more than Himalayan peaks beyond them. At length Ropes—the student who had relieved McTighe at the controls—began to head downward toward the left-hand dark spot whose size marked it as the camp. As he did so, McTighe sent out the last uncensored wireless message the world was to receive from our expedition.

Everyone, of course, has read the brief and unsatisfying bulletins of the rest of our Antarctic sojourn. Some hours after our landing, we sent a guarded report of the tragedy we found, and reluctantly announced the wiping out of the whole Lake party by the frightful wind of the preceding day, or of the night before that. Eleven known dead, young Gedney missing.

People pardoned our hazy lack of details through realization of the shock the sad event must have caused us, and believed us when we explained that the mangling action of the wind had rendered all eleven bodies unsuitable for transportation outside. Indeed, I flatter myself that even in the midst of our distress, utter bewilderment, and soul-clutching horror, we scarcely went beyond the truth in any specific instance. The tremendous significance lies in what we dared not tell; what I would not tell now but for the need of warning others off from nameless terrors.

It is a fact that the wind had brought dreadful havoc. Whether all could have lived through it, even without the other thing, is gravely open to doubt. The storm, with its fury of madly driven ice particles, must have been beyond anything our expedition had encountered before. One aeroplane shelter—all, it seems, had been left in a far too flimsy and inadequate state—was nearly pulverized; and the derrick at the distant boring was entirely shaken to pieces. The exposed metal of the grounded planes and drilling machinery was bruised into a high polish, and two of the small tents were flattened despite their snow banking. Wooden surfaces left out in the blast were pitted and denuded of paint, and all signs of tracks in the snow were completely obliterated. It is also true that we found none of the Archaean biological objects in a condition to take outside as a whole. We did gather some minerals from a vast, tumbled pile, including several of the greenish soapstone fragments whose odd, five-pointed rounding and faint patterns of grouped dots caused so many doubtful comparisons; and some fossil bones, among which were the most typical of the curiously injured specimens.

None of the dogs survived, their hurriedly built snow enclosure near the camp being almost wholly destroyed. The wind may have done that, though the greater breakage on the side next the camp, which was not the windward one, suggests an outward leap or break of the frantic beasts themselves. All three sledges were gone, and we have tried to explain that the wind may have blown them off into the unknown. The drill and ice-melting machinery at the boring were too badly damaged to warrant salvage, so we used them to choke up that subtly disturbing gateway to the past which Lake had blasted. We likewise left at the camp the two most shaken up of the planes; since our surviving party had only four real pilots—Sherman, Danforth, McTighe, and Ropes—in all, with Danforth in a poor nervous shape to navigate. We brought back all the books, scientific equipment, and other incidentals we could find, though much was unaccountably blown away. Spare tents and furs were either missing or badly out of condition.

It was approximately 4 p.m.., after wide plane cruising had forced us to give Gedney up for lost, that we sent our guarded message to the *Arkham* for relaying; and I think we did well to keep it as calm and noncommittal as we succeeded in doing. The most we said about agitation concerned our dogs, whose frantic uneasiness near the biological specimens was to be expected from poor Lake's accounts. We did not mention, I think, their display of the same uneasiness when sniffing around the queer greenish soapstones and certain other objects in the disordered region—objects including scientific instruments, aeroplanes, and machinery, both at the camp and at the boring, whose parts had been loosened, moved, or otherwise tampered with by winds that must have harbored singular curiosity and investigativeness.

About the fourteen biological specimens, we were pardonably indefinite. We said that the only ones we discovered were damaged, but that enough was left of them to prove Lake's description wholly and impressively accurate. It was hard work keeping our personal emotions out of this matter—and we did not mention numbers or say exactly how we had found those which we did find. We had by that time agreed not to transmit anything suggesting madness on the part of Lake's men, and it surely looked like madness to find six imperfect monstrosities carefully buried upright in nine-foot snow graves under five-pointed mounds punched over with groups of dots in patterns exactly those on the queer greenish soapstones dug up from Mesozoic or Tertiary times. The eight perfect specimens mentioned by Lake seemed to have been completely blown away.

We were careful, too, about the public's general peace of mind; hence Danforth and I said little about that frightful trip over the mountains the next day. It was the fact that only a radically lightened plane could possibly cross a range of such height, which mercifully limited that scouting tour to the two of us. On our return at 1 a.m., Danforth was close to hysterics, but kept an admirably stiff upper lip. It took no persuasion to make him promise not to show our sketches and the other things we brought away in our pockets, not to say anything more to the others than what we had agreed to relay outside, and to hide our camera films for private development later on; so that part of my present story will be as new to Pabodie, McTighe, Ropes, Sherman, and the rest as it will be to the world in general. Indeed, Danforth is closer mouthed than I: for he saw, or thinks he saw, one thing he will not tell even me.

As all know, our report included a tale of a hard ascent—a confirmation of Lake's opinion that the great peaks are of Archaean slate and other very primal crumpled strata unchanged since at least middle Comanchian times; a conventional comment on the regularity of the clinging cube and rampart formations; a decision that the cave mouths indicate dissolved calcareous veins; a conjecture that certain slopes and passes would permit of the scaling and crossing of the entire range by seasoned mountaineers; and a remark that the mysterious other side holds a lofty and immense super-plateau as ancient and unchanging as the mountains themselves—twenty thousand feet in elevation, with unsightly rock formations protruding through a thin glacial layer and with low gradual foothills between the general plateau surface and the sheer precipices of the highest peaks.

This body of data is in every respect true so far as it goes, and it completely satisfied the men at the camp. We laid our absence of sixteen hours—a longer time than our announced flying, landing, reconnoitering, and rock-collecting program called for—to a long mythical spell of adverse wind conditions, and told truly of our landing on the farther foothills. Fortunately, our tale sounded realistic and prosaic enough not to tempt any of the others into emulating our flight. Had any tried to do that, I would have used every ounce of my persuasion to stop them—and I do not know what Danforth would have done. While we were gone, Pabodie, Sherman, Ropes, McTighe, and Williamson had worked like beavers over Lake's two best planes, fitting them again for use despite the altogether unaccountable juggling of their operative mechanism.

We decided to load all the planes the next morning and start back for our old base as soon as possible. Even though indirect, that was the safest way to work toward McMurdo Sound; for a straight-line flight across the most utterly unknown stretches of the aeon-dead continent would involve many additional hazards. Further exploration was hardly feasible in view of our tragic decimation and the ruin of our drilling machinery. The doubts and horrors around us—which we did not reveal—made us wish only to escape from this bleak world of desolation and brooding madness as swiftly as we could.

As the public knows, our return to the world was accomplished without further disasters. All planes reached the old base on the evening of the next day—January 27th—after a swift non-stop flight; and on the 28th, we made McMurdo Sound in two laps, the one pause being very brief and occasioned by a faulty rudder in the furious wind over the ice shelf after we had cleared the great plateau. In five days more, the *Arkham* and *Miskatonic*, with all hands and equipment on board, were shaking clear of the thickening field ice and working up Ross Sea with the mocking mountains of Victoria Land looming westward against a troubled Antarctic sky and twisting the wind's wails into a wide-ranged musical piping which chilled my soul to the quick. Less than a fortnight later, we left the last hint of polar land behind us and thanked heaven that we were clear of a haunted, accursed realm where life and death, space and time, have made black and blasphemous alliances, in the unknown epochs since matter first writhed and swam on the planet's scarce-cooled crust.

Since our return, we have all constantly worked to discourage Antarctic exploration, and have kept certain doubts and guesses to ourselves with splendid unity and faithfulness. Even young Danforth, with his nervous breakdown, has not flinched or babbled to his doctors—indeed, as I have said, there is one thing he thinks he alone saw which he will not tell even me, though I think it would help his psychological state if he would consent to do so. It might explain and relieve much, though perhaps the thing was no more than the delusive aftermath of an earlier shock. That is the impression I gather after those rare, irresponsible moments when he whispers disjointed things to me—things which he repudiates vehemently as soon as he gets a grip on himself again.

It will be hard work deterring others from the great white south, and some of our efforts may directly harm our cause by drawing inquiring notice. We might have known from the first that human curiosity is undying, and that the results we announced would be enough to spur others ahead on the same age-long pursuit of the unknown. Lake's reports of those biological monstrosities had aroused naturalists and paleontologists to the highest pitch, though we were sensible enough not to show the detached parts we had taken from the actual buried specimens, or our photographs of those specimens as they were found. We also refrained from showing the more puzzling of the scarred bones and greenish soapstones; while Danforth and I have closely guarded the pictures that we took or drew on the super-plateau across the range, and the crumpled things we smoothed, studied in terror, and brought away in our pockets.

But now that Starkweather-Moore party is organizing, and with a thoroughness far beyond anything our outfit attempted. If not dissuaded, they will get to the innermost nucleus of the Antarctic and melt and bore till they bring up that which we know may end the world. So I must break through all reticences at last—even about that ultimate, nameless thing beyond the mountains of madness.

Chapter 4

It is only with vast hesitancy and repugnance that I let my mind go back to Lake's camp and what we really found there—and to that other thing beyond the mountains of madness. I am constantly tempted to shirk the details, and to let hints stand for actual facts and ineluctable deductions. I hope I have said enough already to let me glide briefly over the rest; the rest, that is, of the horror at the camp. I have told of the wind-ravaged terrain, the damaged shelters, the disarranged machinery, the varied uneasiness of our dogs, the missing sledges and other items, the deaths of men and dogs, the absence of Gedney, and the six insanely buried biological specimens, strangely sound in texture for all their structural injuries, from a world forty million years dead. I do not recall whether I mentioned that upon checking the canine bodies we found one dog missing. We did not think much about that until later—indeed, only Danforth and I have thought of it at all.

The principal things I have been keeping back relate to the bodies, and to certain subtle points which may or may not lend a hideous and incredible kind of rationale to the apparent chaos. At the time, I tried to keep the men's minds off those points; for it was so much simpler—so much more normal—to lay everything to an outbreak of madness on the part of some of Lake's party. From the look of things, that demon mountain wind must have been enough to drive any man mad in the midst of this center of all earthly mystery and desolation.

The crowning abnormality, of course, was the condition of the bodies—men and dogs alike. They had all been in some terrible kind of conflict, and were torn and mangled in fiendish and altogether inexplicable ways. Death, so far as we could judge, had in each case come from strangulation or laceration. The dogs had evidently started the trouble, for the state of their ill-built corral bore witness to its forcible breakage from within. It had been set some distance from the camp because of the hatred of the animals for those hellish Archaean organisms, but the precaution seemed to have been taken in vain. When left alone in that monstrous wind, behind flimsy walls of insufficient height, they must have stampeded—whether from the wind itself or from some subtle, increasing odor emitted by the nightmare specimens, one could not say. Those specimens, of course, had been covered with a tent-cloth; yet the low Antarctic sun had beat steadily upon that cloth, and Lake had mentioned that solar heat tended to make the strangely sound and tough tissues of the things relax and expand. Perhaps the wind had whipped the cloth from over them and jostled them about in such a way that their more pungent olfactory qualities became manifest despite their unbelievable antiquity.

But whatever had happened, it was hideous and revolting enough. Perhaps I had better put squeamishness aside and tell the worst at last—though with a categorical statement of opinion, based on the first-hand observations and most rigid deductions of both Danforth and myself, that the then missing Gedney was in no way responsible for the loathsome horrors we found. I have said that the bodies were frightfully mangled. Now I must add that some were incised and subtracted from in the most curious, cold-blooded, and inhuman fashion. It was the same with dogs and men. All the healthier, fatter bodies, quadrupedal or bipedal, had had their most solid masses of tissue cut out and removed, as by a careful butcher; and around them was a strange sprinkling of salt—taken from the ravaged provision chests on the planes—which conjured up the most horrible associations. The thing had occurred in one of the crude aeroplane shelters from which the plane had been dragged out, and subsequent winds had effaced all tracks which could have supplied any plausible theory. Scattered bits of clothing, roughly slashed from the human incision subjects, hinted no clues. It is useless to bring up the half impression of certain faint snow prints in one shielded corner of the ruined enclosure—because that impression did not concern human prints at all, but was clearly mixed up with all the talk of fossil prints which poor Lake had been giving throughout the preceding weeks. One had to be careful of one's imagination in the lee of those overshadowing mountains of madness.

As I have indicated, Gedney and one dog turned out to be missing in the end. When we came on that terrible shelter, we had missed two dogs and two men; but the fairly unharmed dissecting tent, which we entered after investigating the monstrous graves, had something to reveal. It was not as Lake had left it, for the covered parts of the primal monstrosity had been removed from the improvised table. Indeed, we had already realized that one of the six imperfect and insanely buried things we had found—the one with the trace of a peculiarly hateful odor—must represent the collected sections of the entity which Lake had tried to analyze. On and around that laboratory table were strewn other things, and it did not take long for us to guess that those things were the carefully though oddly and inexpertly dissected parts of one man and one dog. I shall spare the feelings of survivors by omitting mention of the man's identity. Lake's anatomical instruments were missing, but there were evidences of their careful cleansing. The gasoline stove was also gone, though around it we found a curious litter of matches. We buried the human parts beside the other ten men; and the canine parts with the other thirty-five dogs. Concerning the bizarre smudges on the laboratory table, and on the jumble of roughly handled illustrated books scattered near it, we were much too bewildered to speculate.

This formed the worst of the camp horror, but other things were equally perplexing. The disappearance of Gedney, the one dog, the eight uninjured biological specimens, the three sledges, and certain instruments, illustrated technical and scientific books, writing materials, electric torches and batteries, food and fuel, heating apparatus, spare tents, fur suits, and the like, was utterly beyond sane conjecture; as were likewise the spatter-fringed ink blots on certain pieces of paper, and the evidences of curious alien fumbling and experimentation around the planes and all other mechanical devices both at the camp and at the boring. The dogs seemed to abhor this oddly disordered machinery. Then, too, there was the upsetting of the larder, the disappearance of certain staples, and the jarringly comical heap of tin cans pried open in the most unlikely ways and at the most unlikely places. The profusion of scattered matches, intact, broken, or spent, formed another minor enigma—as did the two or three tent cloths and fur suits which we found lying about with peculiar and unorthodox slashings conceivably due to clumsy efforts at unimaginable adaptations. The maltreatment of the human and canine bodies, and the crazy burial of the damaged Archaean specimens, were all of a piece with this apparent disintegrative madness. In view of just such an eventuality as the present one, we carefully photographed all the main evidences of insane disorder at the camp; and shall use the prints to buttress our pleas against the departure of the proposed Starkweather-Moore Expedition.

Our first act after finding the bodies in the shelter was to photograph and open the row of insane graves with the five-pointed snow mounds. We could not help noticing the resemblance of these monstrous mounds, with their clusters of grouped dots, to poor Lake's descriptions of the strange greenish soapstones; and when we came on some of the soapstones themselves in the great mineral pile, we found the likeness very close indeed. The whole general formation, it must be made clear, seemed abominably suggestive of the starfish head of the Archaean entities; and we agreed that the suggestion must have worked potently upon the sensitized minds of Lake's overwrought party. Our own first sight of the actual buried entities formed a horrible moment, and sent the imaginations of Pabodie and myself back to some of the shocking primal myths we had read and heard. We all agreed that the mere sight and continued presence of the things must have cooperated with the oppressive polar solitude and daemon mountain wind in driving Lake's party mad.

For madness—centering in Gedney as the only possible surviving agent—was the explanation spontaneously adopted by everybody so far as spoken utterance was concerned; though I will not be so naive as to deny that each of us may have harbored wild guesses which sanity forbade him to formulate completely. Sherman, Pabodie, and McTighe made an exhaustive aeroplane cruise over all the surrounding territory in the afternoon, sweeping the horizon with field glasses in quest of Gedney and of the various missing things; but nothing came to light. The party reported that the titan barrier range extended endlessly to right and left alike, without any diminution in height or essential structure. On some of the peaks, though, the regular cube and rampart formations were bolder and plainer, having doubly fantastic similitudes to Roerich-painted Asian hill ruins. The distribution of cryptical cave mouths on the black snow-denuded summits seemed roughly even as far as the range could be traced.

In spite of all the prevailing horrors, we were left with enough sheer scientific zeal and adventurousness to wonder about the unknown realm beyond those mysterious mountains. As our guarded messages stated, we rested at midnight after our day of terror and bafflement—but not without a tentative plan for one or more range-crossing altitude flights in a lightened plane with aerial camera and geologist's outfit, beginning the following morning. It was decided that Danforth and I try it first, and we awaked at 7 a.m. intending an early flight; however, heavy winds—mentioned in our brief bulletin to the outside world—delayed our start till nearly nine o'clock.

I have already repeated the noncommittal story we told the men at camp—and relayed outside—after our return sixteen hours later. It is now my terrible duty to amplify this account by filling in the merciful blanks with hints of what we really saw in the hidden transmontane world—hints of the revelations which have finally driven Danforth to a nervous collapse. I wish he would add a really frank word about the thing which he thinks he alone saw—even though it was probably a nervous delusion—and which was perhaps the last straw that put him where he is; but he is firm against that. All I can do is to repeat his later disjointed whispers about what set him shrieking as the plane soared back through the wind-tortured mountain pass after that real and tangible shock which I shared. This will form my last word. If the plain signs of surviving elder horrors in what I disclose be not enough to keep others from meddling with the inner Antarctic—or at least from prying too deeply beneath the surface of that ultimate waste of forbidden secrets and inhuman, aeon-cursed desolation—the responsibility for unnamable and perhaps immeasurable evils will not be mine.

Danforth and I, studying the notes made by Pabodie in his afternoon flight and checking up with a sextant, had calculated that the lowest available pass in the range lay somewhat to the right of us, within sight of camp, and about twenty-three thousand or twenty-four thousand feet above sea level. For this point, then, we first headed in the lightened plane as we embarked on our flight of discovery. The camp itself, on foothills which sprang from a high continental plateau, was some twelve thousand feet in altitude; hence the actual height increase necessary was not so vast as it might seem. Nevertheless, we were acutely conscious of the rarefied air and intense cold as we rose; for, on account of visibility conditions, we had to leave the cabin windows open. We were dressed, of course, in our heaviest furs.

As we drew near the forbidding peaks, dark and sinister above the line of crevasse-riven snow and interstitial glaciers, we noticed more and more the curiously regular formations clinging to the slopes; and thought again of the strange Asian paintings of Nicholas Roerich. The ancient and wind-weathered rock strata fully verified all of Lake's bulletins and proved that these pinnacles had been towering up in exactly the same way since a surprisingly early time in earth's history—perhaps over fifty million years. How much higher they had once been, it was futile to guess; but everything about this strange region pointed to obscure atmospheric influences unfavorable to change and calculated to retard the usual climatic processes of rock disintegration.

But it was the mountainside tangle of regular cubes, ramparts, and cave mouths which fascinated and disturbed us most. I studied them with a field glass and took aerial photographs while Danforth drove; and at times I relieved him at the controls—though my aviation knowledge was purely an amateur's—in order to let him use the binoculars. We could easily see that much of the material of the things was a lightish Archaean quartzite, unlike any formation visible over broad areas of the general surface; and that their regularity was extreme and uncanny to an extent which poor Lake had scarcely hinted.

As he had said, their edges were crumbled and rounded from untold aeons of savage weathering; but their preternatural solidity and tough material had saved them from obliteration. Many parts, especially those closest to the slopes, seemed identical in substance with the surrounding rock surface. The whole arrangement looked like the ruins of Macchu Picchu in the Andes, or the primal foundation walls of Kish as dug up by the Oxford Field Museum Expedition in 1929; and both Danforth and I obtained that occasional impression of *separate Cyclopean blocks* which Lake had attributed to his flight-companion Carroll. How to account for such things in this place was frankly beyond me, and I felt queerly humbled as a geologist. Igneous formations often have strange regularities—like the famous Giants' Causeway in Ireland—but this stupendous range, despite Lake's original suspicion of smoking cones, was above all else non-volcanic in evident structure.

The curious cave mouths, near which the odd formations seemed most abundant, presented another albeit a lesser puzzle because of their regularity of outline. They were, as Lake's bulletin had said, often approximately square or semicircular; as if the natural orifices had been shaped to greater symmetry by some magic hand. Their numerousness and wide distribution were remarkable, and suggested that the whole region was honeycombed with tunnels dissolved out of limestone strata. Such glimpses as we secured did not extend far within the caverns, but we saw that they were apparently clear of stalactites and stalagmites. Outside, those parts of the mountain slopes adjoining the apertures seemed invariably smooth and regular; and Danforth thought that the slight cracks and pittings of the weathering tended toward unusual patterns. Filled as he was with the horrors and strangenesses discovered at the camp, he hinted that the pittings vaguely resembled those baffling groups of dots sprinkled over the primeval greenish soapstones, so hideously duplicated on the madly conceived snow mounds above those six buried monstrosities.

We had risen gradually in flying over the higher foothills and along toward the relatively low pass we had selected. As we advanced, we occasionally looked down at the snow and ice of the land route, wondering whether we could have attempted the trip with the simpler equipment of earlier days. Somewhat to our surprise we saw that the terrain was far from difficult as such things go; and that despite the crevasses and other bad spots, it would not have been likely to deter the sledges of a Scott, a Shackleton, or an Amundsen. Some of the glaciers appeared to lead up to wind-bared passes with unusual continuity, and upon reaching our chosen pass, we found that its case formed no exception.

Our sensations of tense expectancy as we prepared to round the crest and peer out over an untrodden world can hardly be described on paper; even though we had no cause to think the regions beyond the range essentially different from those already seen and traversed. The touch of evil mystery in these barrier mountains, and in the beckoning sea of opalescent sky glimpsed betwixt their summits, was a highly subtle and attenuated matter not to be explained in literal words. Rather was it an affair of vague psychological symbolism and aesthetic association—a thing mixed up with exotic poetry and paintings, and with archaic myths lurking in shunned and forbidden volumes. Even the wind's burden held a peculiar strain of conscious malignity; and for a second, it seemed that the composite sound included a bizarre musical whistling or piping over a wide range as the blast swept in and out of the omnipresent and resonant cave mouths. There was a cloudy note of reminiscent repulsion in this sound, as complex and unplaceable as any of the other dark impressions.

We were now, after a slow ascent, at a height of twenty-three thousand five hundred and seventy feet according to the aneroid, and had left the region of clinging snow definitely below us. Up here were only dark, bare rock slopes and the start of rough-ribbed glaciers—but with those provocative cubes, ramparts, and echoing cave-mouths to add a portent of the unnatural, the fantastic, and the dreamlike. Looking along the line of high peaks, I thought I could see the one mentioned by poor Lake, with a rampart exactly on top. It seemed to be half lost in a queer Antarctic haze—such a haze, perhaps, as had been responsible for Lake's early notion of volcanism. The pass loomed directly before us, smooth and windswept between its jagged and malignly frowning pylons. Beyond it was a sky fretted with swirling vapors and lighted by the low polar sun—the sky of that mysterious farther realm upon which we felt no human eye had ever gazed.

A few more feet of altitude and we would behold that realm. Danforth and I, unable to speak except in shouts amidst the howling, piping wind that raced through the pass and added to the noise of the unmuffled engines, exchanged eloquent glances. And then, having gained those last few feet, we did indeed stare across the momentous divide and over the unsampled secrets of an elder and utterly alien earth.

Chapter 5

I think that both of us simultaneously cried out in mixed awe, wonder, terror, and disbelief in our own senses as we finally cleared the pass and saw what lay beyond. Of course, we must have had some natural theory in the back of our heads to steady our faculties for the moment. Probably we thought of such things as the grotesquely weathered stones of the Garden of the Gods in Colorado, or the fantastically symmetrical wind-carved rocks of the Arizona desert. Perhaps we even half thought the sight a mirage like that we had seen the morning before on first approaching those mountains of madness. We must have had some such normal notions to fall back upon as our eyes swept that limitless, tempest-scarred plateau and grasped the almost endless labyrinth of colossal, regular, and geometrically eurythmic stone masses which reared their crumbled and pitted crests above a glacial sheet not more than forty or fifty feet deep at its thickest, and in places obviously thinner.

The effect of the monstrous sight was indescribable, for some fiendish violation of known natural law seemed certain at the outset. Here, on a hellishly ancient table-land fully twenty thousand feet high, and in a climate deadly to habitation since a pre-human age not less than five hundred thousand years ago, there stretched nearly to the vision's limit a tangle of orderly stone which only the desperation of mental self-defense could possibly attribute to any but a conscious and artificial cause. We had previously dismissed, so far as serious thought was concerned, any theory that the cubes and ramparts of the mountainsides were other than natural in origin. How could they be otherwise, when man himself could scarcely have been differentiated from the great apes at the time when this region succumbed to the present unbroken reign of glacial death?

Yet now the sway of reason seemed irrefutably shaken, for this Cyclopean maze of squared, curved, and angled blocks had features which cut off all comfortable refuge. It was, very clearly, the blasphemous city of the mirage in stark, objective, and ineluctable reality. That damnable portent had had a material basis after all—there had been some horizontal stratum of ice dust in the upper air, and this shocking stone survival had projected its image across the mountains according to the simple laws of reflection, Of course, the phantom had been twisted and exaggerated, and had contained things which the real source did not contain; yet now, as we saw that real source, we thought it even more hideous and menacing than its distant image.

Only the incredible, unhuman massiveness of these vast stone towers and ramparts had saved the frightful things from utter annihilation in the hundreds of thousands—perhaps millions—of years it had brooded there amidst the blasts of a bleak upland. "Corona Mundi—Roof of the World—" All sorts of fantastic phrases sprang to our lips as we looked dizzily down at the unbelievable spectacle. I thought again of the eldritch primal myths that had so persistently haunted me since my first sight of this dead Antarctic world—of the demoniac plateau of Leng, of the Mi-Go, or abominable snowmen of the Himalayas, of the Pnakotic Manuscripts with their pre-human implications, of the Cthulhu cult, of the *Necronomicon*, and of the Hyperborean legends of formless Tsathoggua and the worse than formless star spawn associated with that semi-entity.

For boundless miles in every direction the thing stretched off with very little thinning; indeed, as our eyes followed it to the right and left along the base of the low, gradual foothills which separated it from the actual mountain rim, we decided that we could see no thinning at all except for an interruption at the left of the pass through which we had come. We had merely struck, at random, a limited part of something of incalculable extent. The foothills were more sparsely sprinkled with grotesque stone structures, linking the terrible city to the already familiar cubes and ramparts which evidently formed its mountain outposts. These latter, as well as the queer cave mouths, were as thick on the inner as on the outer sides of the mountains.

The nameless stone labyrinth consisted, for the most part, of walls from ten to one hundred and fifty feet in ice-clear height, and of a thickness varying from five to ten feet. It was composed mostly of prodigious blocks of dark primordial slate, schist, and sandstone—blocks in many cases as large as 4 × 6 × 8 feet—though in several places it seemed to be carved out of a solid, uneven bedrock of pre-Cambrian slate. The buildings were far from equal in size, there being innumerable honeycomb arrangements of enormous extent as well as smaller separate structures. The general shape of these things tended to be conical, pyramidal, or terraced; though there were many perfect cylinders, perfect cubes, clusters of cubes, and other rectangular forms, and a peculiar sprinkling of angled edifices whose five-pointed ground plan roughly suggested modern fortifications. The builders had made constant and expert use of the principle of the arch, and domes had probably existed in the city's heyday.

The whole tangle was monstrously weathered, and the glacial surface from which the towers projected was strewn with fallen blocks and immemorial debris. Where the glaciation was transparent, we could see the lower parts of the gigantic piles, and we noticed the ice-preserved stone bridges which connected the different towers at varying distances above the ground. On the exposed walls we could detect the scarred places where other and higher bridges of the same sort had existed. Closer inspection revealed countless large windows; some of which were closed with shutters of a petrified material originally wood, though most gaped open in a sinister and menacing fashion. Many of the ruins, of course, were roofless, and with uneven though wind-rounded upper edges; whilst others, of a more sharply conical or pyramidal model or else protected by higher surrounding structures, preserved intact outlines despite the omnipresent crumbling and pitting. With the field glass we could barely make out what seemed to be sculptural decorations in horizontal bands—decorations including those curious groups of dots whose presence on the ancient soapstones now assumed a vastly larger significance.

In many places, the buildings were totally ruined and the ice sheet deeply riven from various geologic causes. In other places, the stonework was worn down to the very level of the glaciation. One broad swath, extending from the plateau's interior, to a cleft in the foothills about a mile to the left of the pass we had traversed, was wholly free from buildings. It probably represented, we concluded, the course of some great river which in Tertiary times—millions of years ago—had poured through the city and into some prodigious subterranean abyss of the great barrier range. Certainly, this was above all a region of caves, gulfs, and underground secrets beyond human penetration.

Looking back to our sensations, and recalling our dazedness at viewing this monstrous survival from aeons we had thought pre-human, I can only wonder that we preserved the semblance of equilibrium, which we did. Of course, we knew that something—chronology, scientific theory, or our own consciousness—was woefully awry; yet, we kept enough poise to guide the plane, observe many things quite minutely, and take a careful series of photographs which may yet serve both us and the world in good stead. In my case, ingrained scientific habit may have helped; for above all my bewilderment and sense of menace, there burned a dominant curiosity to fathom more of this age-old secret—to know what sort of beings had built and lived in this incalculably gigantic place, and what relation to the general world of its time or of other times so unique a concentration of life could have had.

For this place could be no ordinary city. It must have formed the primary nucleus and center of some archaic and unbelievable chapter of earth's history whose outward ramifications, recalled only dimly in the most obscure and distorted myths, had vanished utterly amidst the chaos of terrene convulsions long before any human race we know had shambled out of apedom. Here sprawled a Palaeogaean megalopolis compared with which the fabled Atlantis and Lemuria, Commoriom and Uzuldaroum, and Olathoë in the land of Lomar, are recent things of today—not even of yesterday; a megalopolis ranking with such whispered pre-human blasphemies as Valusia, R'lyeh, Ib in the land of Mnar, and the Nameless city of Arabia Deserta. As we flew above that tangle of stark titan towers, my imagination sometimes escaped all bounds and roved aimlessly in realms of fantastic associations—even weaving links betwixt this lost world and some of my own wildest dreams concerning the mad horror at the camp.

The plane's fuel tank, in the interest of greater lightness, had been only partly filled; hence we now had to exert caution in our explorations. Even so, however, we covered an enormous extent of ground—or, rather, air—after swooping down to a level where the wind became virtually negligible. There seemed to be no limit to the mountain range, or to the length of the frightful stone city which bordered its inner foothills. Fifty miles of flight in each direction showed no major change in the labyrinth of rock and masonry that clawed up corpse-like through the eternal ice. There were, though, some highly absorbing diversifications; such as the carvings on the canyon where that broad river had once pierced the foothills and approached its sinking place in the great range. The headlands at the stream's entrance had been boldly carved into Cyclopean pylons; and something about the ridgy, barrel-shaped designs stirred up oddly vague, hateful, and confusing semi-remembrances in both Danforth and me.

We also came upon several star-shaped open spaces, evidently public squares, and noted various undulations in the terrain. Where a sharp hill rose, it was generally hollowed out into some sort of rambling stone edifice; but there were at least two exceptions. Of these latter, one was too badly weathered to disclose what had been on the jutting eminence, while the other still bore a fantastic conical monument carved out of the solid rock and roughly resembling such things as the well-known Snake Tomb in the ancient valley of Petra.

Flying inland from the mountains, we discovered that the city was not of infinite width, even though its length along the foothills seemed endless. After about thirty miles the grotesque stone buildings began to thin out, and in ten more miles we came to an unbroken waste virtually without signs of sentient artifice. The course of the river beyond the city seemed marked by a broad, depressed line, while the land assumed a somewhat greater ruggedness, seeming to slope slightly upward as it receded in the mist-hazed west.

So far we had made no landing, yet to leave the plateau without an attempt at entering some of the monstrous structures would have been inconceivable. Accordingly, we decided to find a smooth place on the foothills near our navigable pass, there grounding the plane and preparing to do some exploration on foot. Though these gradual slopes were partly covered with a scattering of ruins, low flying soon disclosed an ample number of possible landing-places. Selecting that nearest to the pass, since our flight would be across the great range and back to camp, we succeeded about 12:30 p.m. in effecting a landing on a smooth, hard snowfield wholly devoid of obstacles and well adapted to a swift and favorable takeoff later on.

It did not seem necessary to protect the plane with a snow banking for so brief a time and in so comfortable an absence of high winds at this level; hence, we merely saw that the landing skis were safely lodged, and that the vital parts of the mechanism were guarded against the cold. For our foot journey we discarded the heaviest of our flying furs, and took with us a small outfit consisting of pocket compass, hand camera, light provisions, voluminous notebooks and paper, geologist's hammer and chisel, specimen-bags, coil of climbing rope, and powerful electric torches with extra batteries; this equipment having been carried in the plane on the chance that we might be able to effect a landing, take ground pictures, make drawings and topographical sketches, and obtain rock specimens from some bare slope, outcropping, or mountain cave. Fortunately, we had a supply of extra paper to tear up, place in a spare specimen-bag, and use on the ancient principle of hare-and-hounds for marking our course in any interior mazes we might be able to penetrate. This had been brought in case we found some cave system with air quiet enough to allow such a rapid and easy method in place of the usual rock-chipping method of trailblazing.

Walking cautiously downhill over the crusted snow toward the stupendous stone labyrinth that loomed against the opalescent west, we felt almost as keen a sense of imminent marvels as we had felt on approaching the unfathomed mountain pass four hours previously. True, we had become visually familiar with the incredible secret concealed by the barrier peaks; yet the prospect of actually entering primordial walls reared by conscious beings perhaps millions of years ago—before any known race of men could have existed—was none the less awesome and potentially terrible in its implications of cosmic abnormality. Though the thinness of the air at this prodigious altitude made exertion somewhat more difficult than usual, both Danforth and I found ourselves bearing up very well, and felt equal to almost any task which might fall to our lot. It took only a few steps to bring us to a shapeless ruin worn level with the snow, while ten or fifteen rods farther on there was a huge, roofless rampart still complete in its gigantic, five-pointed outline and rising to an irregular height of ten or eleven feet. For this latter we headed; and when at last we were actually able to touch its weathered Cyclopean blocks, we felt that we had established an unprecedented and almost blasphemous link with forgotten aeons normally closed to our species.

This rampart, shaped like a star and perhaps three hundred feet from point to point, was built of Jurassic sandstone blocks of irregular size, averaging 6×8 feet in surface. There was a row of arched loopholes or windows about four feet wide and five feet high, spaced quite symmetrically along the points of the star and at its inner angles, and with the bottoms about four feet from the glaciated surface. Looking through these, we could see that the masonry was fully five feet thick, that there were no partitions remaining within, and that there were traces of banded carvings or bas-reliefs on the interior walls—facts we had indeed guessed before, when flying low over this rampart and others like it. Though lower parts must have originally existed, all traces of such things were now wholly obscured by the deep layer of ice and snow at this point.

We crawled through one of the windows and vainly tried to decipher the nearly effaced mural designs, but did not attempt to disturb the glaciated floor. Our orientation flights had indicated that many buildings in the city proper were less ice-choked, and that we might perhaps find wholly clear interiors leading down to the true ground level if we entered those structures still roofed at the top. Before we left the rampart, we photographed it carefully and studied its mortarless Cyclopean masonry with complete bewilderment. We wished that Pabodie were present, for his engineering knowledge might have helped us guess how such titanic blocks could have been handled in that unbelievably remote age when the city and its outskirts were built up.

The half-mile walk downhill to the actual city, with the upper wind shrieking vainly and savagely through the skyward peaks in the background, was something of which the smallest details will always remain engraved on my mind. Only in fantastic nightmares could any human beings but Danforth and me conceive such optical effects. Between us and the churning vapors of the west lay that monstrous tangle of dark stone towers, its outré and incredible forms impressing us afresh at every new angle of vision. It was a mirage in solid stone, and were it not for the photographs, I would still doubt that such a thing could be. The general type of masonry was identical with that of the rampart we had examined; but the extravagant shapes which this masonry took in its urban manifestations were past all description.

Even the pictures illustrate only one or two phases of its endless variety, preternatural massiveness, and utterly alien exoticism. There were geometrical forms for which a Euclid would scarcely find a name—cones of all degrees of irregularity and truncation, terraces of every sort of provocative disproportion, shafts with odd bulbous enlargements, broken columns in curious groups, and five-pointed or five-ridged arrangements of mad grotesqueness. As we drew nearer, we could see beneath certain transparent parts of the ice-sheet, and detect some of the tubular stone bridges that connected the crazily sprinkled structures at various heights. Of orderly streets there seemed to be none, the only broad open swath being a mile to the left, where the ancient river had doubtless flowed through the town into the mountains.

Our field-glasses showed the external, horizontal bands of nearly effaced sculptures and dot-groups to be very prevalent, and we could half imagine what the city must once have looked like—even though most of the roofs and tower tops had necessarily perished. As a whole, it had been a complex tangle of twisted lanes and alleys, all of them deep canyons, and some little better than tunnels because of the overhanging masonry or over-arching bridges. Now, outspread below us, it loomed like a dream fantasy against a westward mist through whose northern end the low, reddish Antarctic sun of early afternoon was struggling to shine; and when, for a moment, that sun encountered a denser obstruction and plunged the scene into temporary shadow, the effect was subtly menacing in a way I can never hope to depict. Even the faint howling and piping of the unfelt wind in the great mountain passes behind us took on a wilder note of purposeful malignity. The last stage of our descent to the town was unusually steep and abrupt, and a rock outcropping at the edge where the grade changed led us to think that an artificial terrace had once existed there. Under the glaciation, we believed, there must be a flight of steps or its equivalent.

When at last we plunged into the town itself, clambering over fallen masonry and shrinking from the oppressive nearness and dwarfing height of omnipresent crumbling and pitted walls, our sensations again became such that I marvel at the amount of self-control we retained. Danforth was frankly jumpy and began making some offensively irrelevant speculations about the horror at the camp—which I resented all the more because I could not help sharing certain conclusions forced upon us by many features of this morbid survival from nightmare antiquity. The speculations worked on his imagination, too; for in one place—where a debris-littered alley turned a sharp corner—he insisted that he saw faint traces of ground markings which he did not like; whilst elsewhere he stopped to listen to a subtle, imaginary sound from some undefined point—a muffled musical piping, he said, not unlike that of the wind in the mountain caves, yet somehow disturbingly different. The ceaseless *five-pointedness* of the surrounding architecture and of the few distinguishable mural arabesques had a dimly sinister suggestiveness we could not escape, and gave us a touch of terrible subconscious certainty concerning the primal entities which had reared and dwelt in this unhallowed place.

Nevertheless, our scientific and adventurous souls were not wholly dead, and we mechanically carried out our program of chipping specimens from all the different rock types represented in the masonry. We wished a rather full set in order to draw better conclusions regarding the age of the place. Nothing in the great outer walls seemed to date from later than the Jurassic and Comanchian periods, nor was any piece of stone in the entire place of a greater recency than the Pliocene Age. In stark certainty, we were wandering amidst a death which had reigned at least five hundred thousand years, and in all probability even longer.

As we proceeded through this maze of stone-shadowed twilight we stopped at all available apertures to study interiors and investigate entrance possibilities. Some were above our reach, whilst others led only into ice-choked ruins as unroofed and barren as the rampart on the hill. One, though spacious and inviting, opened on a seemingly bottomless abyss without visible means of descent. Now and then we had a chance to study the petrified wood of a surviving shutter and were impressed by the fabulous antiquity implied in the still discernible grain. These things had come from Mesozoic gymnosperms and conifers—especially Cretaceous cycads—and from fan palms and early angiosperms of plainly Tertiary date. Nothing definitely later than the Pliocene could be discovered. In the placing of these shutters—whose edges showed the former presence of queer and long-vanished hinges—usage seemed to be varied—some being on the outer and some on the inner side of the deep embrasures. They seemed to have become wedged in place, thus surviving the rusting of their former and probably metallic fixtures and fastenings.

After a time, we came across a row of windows—in the bulges of a colossal five-edged cone of undamaged apex—which led into a vast, well-preserved room with stone flooring; but these were too high in the room to permit descent without a rope. We had a rope with us, but did not wish to bother with this twenty-foot drop unless obliged to—especially in this thin plateau air where great demands were made upon the heart action. This enormous room was probably a hall or concourse of some sort, and our electric torches showed bold, distinct, and potentially startling sculptures arranged round the walls in broad, horizontal bands separated by equally broad strips of conventional arabesques. We took careful note of this spot, planning to enter here unless a more easily gained interior were encountered.

Finally, though, we did encounter exactly the opening we wished; an archway about six feet wide and ten feet high, marking the former end of an aerial bridge which had spanned an alley about five feet above the present level of glaciation. These archways, of course, were flush with upper-story floors, and in this case one of the floors still existed. The building thus accessible was a series of rectangular terraces on our left facing westward. That across the alley, where the other archway yawned, was a decrepit cylinder with no windows and with a curious bulge about ten feet above the aperture. It was totally dark inside, and the archway seemed to open on a well of illimitable emptiness.

Heaped debris made the entrance to the vast left-hand building doubly easy; yet, for a moment we hesitated before taking advantage of the long-wished chance. For though we had penetrated into this tangle of archaic mystery, it required fresh resolution to carry us actually inside a complete and surviving building of a fabulous elder world whose nature was becoming more and more hideously plain to us. In the end, however, we made the plunge, and scrambled up over the rubble into the gaping embrasure. The floor beyond was of great slate slabs, and seemed to form the outlet of a long, high corridor with sculptured walls.

Observing the many inner archways which led off from it, and realizing the probable complexity of the nest of apartments within, we decided that we must begin our system of hare-and-hound trailblazing. Hitherto our compasses, together with frequent glimpses of the vast mountain range between the towers in our rear, had been enough to prevent our losing our way; but from now on, the artificial substitute would be necessary. Accordingly, we reduced our extra paper to shreds of suitable size, placed these in a bag to be carried by Danforth, and prepared to use them as economically as safety would allow. This method would probably gain us immunity from straying, since there did not appear to be any strong air currents inside the primordial masonry. If such should develop, or if our paper supply should give out, we could of course fall back on the more secure though more tedious and retarding method of rock-chipping.

Just how extensive a territory we had opened up, it was impossible to guess without a trial. The close and frequent connection of the different buildings made it likely that we might cross from one to another on bridges underneath the ice, except where impeded by local collapses and geologic rifts, for very little glaciation seemed to have entered the massive constructions. Almost all the areas of transparent ice had revealed the submerged windows as tightly shuttered, as if the town had been left in that uniform state until the glacial sheet came to crystallize the lower part for all succeeding time. Indeed, one gained a curious impression that this place had been deliberately closed and deserted in some dim, bygone aeon, rather than overwhelmed by any sudden calamity or even gradual decay. Had the coming of the ice been foreseen, and had a nameless population left en masse to seek a less doomed abode? The precise physiographic conditions attending the formation of the ice-sheet at this point would have to wait for later solution. It had not, very plainly, been a grinding drive. Perhaps the pressure of accumulated snows had been responsible, and perhaps some flood from the river, or from the bursting of some ancient glacial dam in the great range, had helped to create the special state now observable. Imagination could conceive almost anything in connection with this place.

Chapter 6

It would be cumbrous to give a detailed, consecutive account of our wanderings inside that cavernous, aeon-dead honeycomb of primal masonry—that monstrous lair of elder secrets which now echoed for the first time, after uncounted epochs, to the tread of human feet. This is especially true because so much of the horrible drama and revelation came from a mere study of the omnipresent mural carvings. Our flashlight photographs of those carvings will do much toward proving the truth of what we are now disclosing, and it is lamentable that we had not a larger film supply with us. As it was, we made crude notebook sketches of certain salient features after all our films were used up.

The building which we had entered was one of great size and elaborateness, and gave us an impressive notion of the architecture of that nameless geologic past. The inner partitions were less massive than the outer walls, but on the lower levels were excellently preserved. Labyrinthine complexity, involving curiously irregular differences in floor levels, characterized the entire arrangement; and we should certainly have been lost at the very outset but for the trail of torn paper left behind us. We decided to explore the more decrepit upper parts first of all, hence climbed aloft in the maze for a distance of some one hundred feet, to where the topmost tier of chambers yawned snowily and ruinously open to the polar sky. Ascent was effected over the steep, transversely ribbed stone ramps or inclined planes which everywhere served in lieu of stairs. The rooms we encountered were of all imaginable shapes and proportions, ranging from five-pointed stars to triangles and perfect cubes. It might be safe to say that their general average was about 30 × 30 feet in floor area, and 20 feet in height, though many larger apartments existed. After thoroughly examining the upper regions and the glacial level, we descended, story by story, into the submerged part, where indeed we soon saw we were in a continuous maze of connected chambers and passages probably leading over unlimited areas outside this particular building. The Cyclopean massiveness and gigantism of everything about us became curiously oppressive; and there was something vaguely but deeply unhuman in all the contours, dimensions, proportions, decorations, and constructional nuances of the blasphemously archaic stonework. We soon realized, from what the carvings revealed, that this monstrous city was many million years old.

We cannot yet explain the engineering principles used in the anomalous balancing and adjustment of the vast rock masses, though the function of the arch was clearly much relied on. The rooms we visited were wholly bare of all portable contents, a circumstance which sustained our belief in the city's deliberate desertion. The prime decorative feature was the almost universal system of mural sculpture, which tended to run in continuous horizontal bands three feet wide and arranged from floor to ceiling in alternation with bands of equal width given over to geometrical arabesques. There were exceptions to this rule of arrangement, but its preponderance was overwhelming. Often, however, a series of smooth cartouches containing oddly patterned groups of dots would be sunk along one of the arabesque bands.

The technique, we soon saw, was mature, accomplished, and aesthetically evolved to the highest degree of civilized mastery, though utterly alien in every detail to any known art tradition of the human race. In delicacy of execution no sculpture I have ever seen could approach it. The minutest details of elaborate vegetation, or of animal life, were rendered with astonishing vividness despite the bold scale of the carvings; whilst the conventional designs were marvels of skillful intricacy. The arabesques displayed a profound use of mathematical principles, and were made up of obscurely symmetrical curves and angles based on the quantity of five. The pictorial bands followed a highly formalized tradition, and involved a peculiar treatment of perspective, but had an artistic force that moved us profoundly, notwithstanding the intervening gulf of vast geologic periods. Their method of design hinged on a singular juxtaposition of the cross-section with the two-dimensional silhouette, and embodied an analytical psychology beyond that of any known race of antiquity. It is useless to try to compare this art with any represented in our museums. Those who see our photographs will probably find its closest analogue in certain grotesque conceptions of the most daring futurists.

The arabesque tracery consisted altogether of depressed lines, whose depth on unweathered walls varied from one to two inches. When cartouches with dot-groups appeared—evidently as inscriptions in some unknown and primordial language and alphabet—the depression of the smooth surface was perhaps an inch and a half, and of the dots perhaps a half inch more. The pictorial bands were in countersunk low relief, their background being depressed about two inches from the original wall surface. In some specimens, marks of a former coloration could be detected, though for the most part the untold aeons had disintegrated and banished any pigments which may have been applied. The more one studied the marvelous technique, the more one admired the things. Beneath their strict conventionalization, one could grasp the minute and accurate observation and graphic skill of the artists; and indeed, the very conventions themselves served to symbolize and accentuate the real essence or vital differentiation of every object delineated. We felt, too, that besides these recognizable excellences there were others lurking beyond the reach of our perceptions. Certain touches here and there gave vague hints of latent symbols and stimuli which another mental and emotional background, and a fuller or different sensory equipment, might have made of profound and poignant significance to us.

The subject matter of the sculptures obviously came from the life of the vanished epoch of their creation, and contained a large proportion of evident history. It is this abnormal historic-mindedness of the primal race—a chance circumstance operating, through coincidence, miraculously in our favor—which made the carvings so awesomely informative to us, and which caused us to place their photography and transcription above all other considerations. In certain rooms the dominant arrangement was varied by the presence of maps, astronomical charts, and other scientific designs of an enlarged scale—these things giving a naive and terrible corroboration to what we gathered from the pictorial friezes and dadoes. In hinting at what the whole revealed, I can only hope that my account will not arouse a curiosity greater than sane caution on the part of those who believe me at all. It would be tragic if any were to be allured to that realm of death and horror by the very warning meant to discourage them.

Interrupting these sculptured walls were high windows and massive twelve-foot doorways; both now and then retaining the petrified wooden planks—elaborately carved and polished—of the actual shutters and doors. All metal fixtures had long ago vanished, but some of the doors remained in place and had to be forced aside as we progressed from room to room. Window-frames with odd transparent panes—mostly elliptical—survived here and there, though in no considerable quantity. There were also frequent niches of great magnitude, generally empty, but once in a while containing some bizarre object carved from green soapstone which was either broken or perhaps held too inferior to warrant removal. Other apertures were undoubtedly connected with bygone mechanical facilities—heating, lighting, and the like—of a sort suggested in many of the carvings. Ceilings tended to be plain, but had sometimes been inlaid with green soapstone or other tiles, mostly fallen now. Floors were also paved with such tiles, though plain stonework predominated.

As I have said, all furniture and other movables were absent; but the sculptures gave a clear idea of the strange devices which had once filled these tomb-like, echoing rooms. Above the glacial sheet, the floors were generally thick with detritus, litter, and debris; but farther down, this condition decreased. In some of the lower chambers and corridors, there was little more than gritty dust or ancient incrustations, while occasional areas had an uncanny air of newly swept immaculateness. Of course, where rifts or collapses had occurred, the lower levels were as littered as the upper ones. A central court—as in other structures we had seen from the air—saved the inner regions from total darkness; so that we seldom had to use our electric torches in the upper rooms except when studying sculptured details. Below the ice cap, however, the twilight deepened; and in many parts of the tangled ground level there was an approach to absolute blackness.

To form even a rudimentary idea of our thoughts and feelings as we penetrated this aeon-silent maze of unhuman masonry, one must correlate a hopelessly bewildering chaos of fugitive moods, memories, and impressions. The sheer appalling antiquity and lethal desolation of the place were enough to overwhelm almost any sensitive person, but added to these elements were the recent unexplained horror at the camp, and the revelations all too soon effected by the terrible mural sculptures around us. The moment we came upon a perfect section of carving, where no ambiguity of interpretation could exist, it took only a brief study to give us the hideous truth—a truth which it would be naive to claim Danforth and I had not independently suspected before, though we had carefully refrained from even hinting it to each other. There could now be no further merciful doubt about the nature of the beings which had built and inhabited this monstrous dead city millions of years ago, when man's ancestors were primitive archaic mammals, and vast dinosaurs roamed the tropical steppes of Europe and Asia.

We had previously clung to a desperate alternative and insisted—each to himself—that the omnipresence of the five-pointed motifs meant only some cultural or religious exaltation of the Archaean natural object which had so patently embodied the quality of five-pointedness; as the decorative motifs of Minoan Crete exalted the sacred bull, those of Egypt the scarabaeus, those of Rome the wolf and the eagle, and those of various savage tribes some chosen totem animal. But this lone refuge was now stripped from us, and we were forced to face definitely the reason-shaking realization which the reader of these pages has doubtless long ago anticipated. I can scarcely bear to write it down in black and white even now, but perhaps that will not be necessary.

The things once rearing and dwelling in this frightful masonry in the age of dinosaurs were not dinosaurs, but far worse. Mere dinosaurs were new and almost brainless objects—but the builders of the city were wise and old, and had left certain traces in rocks even then laid down well nigh a thousand million years—rocks laid down before the true life of earth had advanced beyond plastic groups of cells—rocks laid down before the true life of earth had existed at all. They were the makers and enslavers of that life, and above all doubt the originals of the fiendish elder myths which things like the Pnakotic Manuscripts and the *Necronomicon* affrightedly hint about. They were the great "Old Ones" that had filtered down from the stars when earth was young—the beings whose substance an alien evolution had shaped, and whose powers were such as this planet had never bred. And to think that only the day before Danforth and I had actually looked upon fragments of their millennially fossilized substance—and that poor Lake and his party had seen their complete outlines.

It is of course impossible for me to relate in proper order the stages by which we picked up what we know of that monstrous chapter of pre-human life. After the first shock of the certain revelation, we had to pause a while to recuperate, and it was fully three o'clock before we got started on our actual tour of systematic research. The sculptures in the building we entered were of relatively late date—perhaps two million years ago—as checked up by geological, biological, and astronomical features—and embodied an art which would be called decadent in comparison with that of specimens we found in older buildings after crossing bridges under the glacial sheet. One edifice hewn from the solid rock seemed to go back forty or possibly even fifty million years—to the lower Eocene or upper Cretaceous—and contained bas-reliefs of an artistry surpassing anything else, with one tremendous exception, that we encountered. That was, we have since agreed, the oldest domestic structure we traversed.

Were it not for the support of those photographs soon to be made public, I would refrain from telling what I found and inferred, lest I be confined as a madman. Of course, the infinitely early parts of the patchwork tale—representing the pre-terrestrial life of the star-headed beings on other planets, in other galaxies, and in other universes—can readily be interpreted as the fantastic mythology of those beings themselves; yet such parts sometimes involved designs and diagrams so uncannily close to the latest findings of mathematics and astrophysics that I scarcely know what to think. Let others judge when they see the photographs I shall publish.

Naturally, no one set of carvings which we encountered told more than a fraction of any connected story, nor did we even begin to come upon the various stages of that story in their proper order. Some of the vast rooms were independent units so far as their designs were concerned, whilst in other cases a continuous chronicle would be carried through a series of rooms and corridors. The best of the maps and diagrams were on the walls of a frightful abyss below even the ancient ground level—a cavern perhaps two hundred feet square and sixty feet high, which had almost undoubtedly been an educational center of some sort. There were many provoking repetitions of the same material in different rooms and buildings, since certain chapters of experience, and certain summaries or phases of racial history, had evidently been favorites with different decorators or dwellers. Sometimes, though, variant versions of the same theme proved useful in settling debatable points and filling up gaps.

I still wonder that we deduced so much in the short time at our disposal. Of course, we even now have only the barest outline—and much of that was obtained later on from a study of the photographs and sketches we made. It may be the effect of this later study—the revived memories and vague impressions acting in conjunction with his general sensitiveness and with that final supposed horror-glimpse whose essence he will not reveal even to me—which has been the immediate source of Danforth's present breakdown. But it had to be; for we could not issue our warning intelligently without the fullest possible information, and the issuance of that warning is a prime necessity. Certain lingering influences in that unknown Antarctic world of disordered time and alien natural law make it imperative that further exploration be discouraged.

Chapter 7

The full story, so far as deciphered, will eventually appear in an official bulletin of Miskatonic University. Here I shall sketch only the salient highlights in a formless, rambling way. Myth or otherwise, the sculptures told of the coming of those star-headed things to the nascent, lifeless earth out of cosmic space—their coming, and the coming of many other alien entities such as at certain times embark upon spatial pioneering. They seemed able to traverse the interstellar ether on their vast membranous wings—thus oddly confirming some curious hill folklore long ago told me by an antiquarian colleague. They had lived under the sea a good deal, building fantastic cities and fighting terrific battles with nameless adversaries by means of intricate devices employing unknown principles of energy. Evidently their scientific and mechanical knowledge far surpassed man's today, though they made use of its more widespread and elaborate forms only when obliged to do so. Some of the sculptures suggested that they had passed through a stage of mechanized life on other planets, but had receded upon finding its effects emotionally unsatisfying. Their preternatural toughness of organization and simplicity of natural wants made them peculiarly able to live on a high plane without the more specialized fruits of artificial manufacture, and even without garments, except for occasional protection against the elements.

It was under the sea, at first for food and later for other purposes, that they first created earth-life—using available substances according to long-known methods. The more elaborate experiments came after the annihilation of various cosmic enemies. They had done the same thing on other planets, having manufactured not only necessary foods, but certain multicellular protoplasmic masses capable of molding their tissues into all sorts of temporary organs under hypnotic influence and thereby forming ideal slaves to perform the heavy work of the community. These viscous masses were without doubt what Abdul Alhazred whispered about as "Shoggoths" in his frightful *Necronomicon*, though even that mad Arab had not hinted that any existed on earth except in the dreams of those who had chewed a certain alkaloidal herb. When the star-headed Old Ones on this planet had synthesized their simple food forms and bred a good supply of Shoggoths, they allowed other cell-groups to develop into other forms of animal and vegetable life for sundry purposes, extirpating any whose presence became troublesome.

With the aid of the Shoggoths, whose expansions could be made to lift prodigious weights, the small, low cities under the sea grew to vast and imposing labyrinths of stone not unlike those which later rose on land. Indeed, the highly adaptable Old Ones had lived much on land in other parts of the universe, and probably retained many traditions of land construction. As we studied the architecture of all these sculptured palaeogean cities, including that whose aeon-dead corridors we were even then traversing, we were impressed by a curious coincidence which we have not yet tried to explain, even to ourselves. The tops of the buildings, which in the actual city around us had, of course, been weathered into shapeless ruins ages ago, were clearly displayed in the bas-reliefs, and showed vast clusters of needle-like spires, delicate finials on certain cone and pyramid apexes and tiers of thin, horizontal scalloped disks capping cylindrical shafts. This was exactly what we had seen in that monstrous and portentous mirage, cast by a dead city whence such skyline features had been absent for thousands and tens of thousands of years, which loomed on our ignorant eyes across the unfathomed mountains of madness as we first approached poor Lake's ill-fated camp.

Of the life of the Old Ones, both under the sea and after part of them migrated to land, volumes could be written. Those in shallow water had continued the fullest use of the eyes at the ends of their five main head tentacles, and had practiced the arts of sculpture and of writing in quite the usual way—the writing accomplished with a stylus on waterproof waxen surfaces. Those lower down in the ocean depths, though they used a curious phosphorescent organism to furnish light, pieced out their vision with obscure special senses operating through the prismatic cilia on their heads—senses which rendered all the Old Ones partly independent of light in emergencies. Their forms of sculpture and writing had changed curiously during the descent, embodying certain apparently chemical coating processes—probably to secure phosphorescence—which the bas-reliefs could not make clear to us. The beings moved in the sea partly by swimming—using the lateral crinoid arms—and partly by wriggling with the lower tier of tentacles containing the pseudo-feet. Occasionally, they accomplished long swoops with the auxiliary use of two or more sets of their fan-like folding wings. On land they locally used the pseudo-feet, but now and then flew to great heights or over long distances with their wings. The many slender tentacles into which the crinoid arms branched were infinitely delicate, flexible, strong, and accurate in muscular-nervous coordination—ensuring the utmost skill and dexterity in all artistic and other manual operations.

The toughness of the things was almost incredible. Even the terrific pressure of the deepest sea-bottoms appeared powerless to harm them.

Very few seemed to die at all except by violence, and their burial places were very limited. The fact that they covered their vertically inhumed dead with five-pointed inscribed mounds set up thoughts in Danforth and me which made a fresh pause and recuperation necessary after the sculptures revealed it. The beings multiplied by means of spores—like vegetable pteridophytes, as Lake had suspected—but, owing to their prodigious toughness and longevity, and consequent lack of replacement needs, they did not encourage the large-scale development of new prothallia except when they had new regions to colonize. The young matured swiftly and received an education evidently beyond any standard we can imagine. The prevailing intellectual and aesthetic life was highly evolved, and produced a tenaciously enduring set of customs and institutions which I shall describe more fully in my coming monograph. These varied slightly according to sea or land residence, but had the same foundations and essentials.

Though able, like vegetables, to derive nourishment from inorganic substances, they vastly preferred organic and especially animal food. They ate uncooked marine life under the sea, but cooked their viands on land. They hunted game and raised meat herds—slaughtering with sharp weapons whose odd marks on certain fossil bones our expedition had noted. They resisted all ordinary temperatures marvelously, and in their natural state could live in water down to freezing. When the great chill of the Pleistocene drew on, however—nearly a million years ago—the land dwellers had to resort to special measures, including artificial heating—until at last the deadly cold appears to have driven them back into the sea. For their prehistoric flights through cosmic space, legend said, they absorbed certain chemicals and became almost independent of eating, breathing, or heat conditions—but by the time of the great cold, they had lost track of the method. In any case, they could not have prolonged the artificial state indefinitely without harm.

Being non-pairing and semi-vegetable in structure, the Old Ones had no biological basis for the family phase of mammal life, but seemed to organize large households on the principles of comfortable space-utility and—as we deduced from the pictured occupations and diversions of co-dwellers—congenial mental association. In furnishing their homes, they kept everything in the center of the huge rooms, leaving all the wall spaces free for decorative treatment. Lighting, in the case of the land inhabitants, was accomplished by a device, probably electro-chemical in nature. Both on land and under water, they used curious tables, chairs, and couches like cylindrical frames—for they rested and slept upright with folded-down tentacles—and racks for hinged sets of dotted surfaces forming their books.

Government was evidently complex and probably socialistic, though no certainties in this regard could be deduced from the sculptures we saw.

There was extensive commerce, both local and between different cities—certain small, flat counters, five-pointed and inscribed, serving as money. Probably the smaller of the various greenish soapstones found by our expedition were pieces of such currency. Though the culture was mainly urban, some agriculture and much stock raising existed. Mining and a limited amount of manufacturing were also practiced. Travel was very frequent, but permanent migration seemed relatively rare except for the vast colonizing movements by which the race expanded. For personal locomotion, no external aid was used, since in land, air, and water movement alike the Old Ones seemed to possess excessively vast capacities for speed. Loads, however, were drawn by beasts of burden—Shoggoths under the sea, and a curious variety of primitive vertebrates in the later years of land existence.

These vertebrates, as well as an infinity of other life forms—animal and vegetable, marine, terrestrial, and aerial—were the products of unguided evolution acting on life cells made by the Old Ones, but escaping beyond their radius of attention. They had been suffered to develop unchecked because they had not come in conflict with the dominant beings. Bothersome forms, of course, were mechanically exterminated. It interested us to see in some of the very last and most decadent sculptures a shambling, primitive mammal, used sometimes for food and sometimes as an amusing buffoon by the land dwellers, whose vaguely simian and human foreshadowings were unmistakable. In the building of land cities, the huge stone blocks of the high towers were generally lifted by vast-winged pterodactyls of a species heretofore unknown to paleontology.

The persistence with which the Old Ones survived various geologic changes and convulsions of the earth's crust was little short of miraculous. Though few or none of their first cities seem to have remained beyond the Archaean Age, there was no interruption in their civilization or in the transmission of their records. Their original place of advent to the planet was the Antarctic Ocean, and it is likely that they came not long after the matter forming the moon was wrenched from the neighboring South Pacific. According to one of the sculptured maps the whole globe was then under water, with stone cities scattered farther and farther from the Antarctic as aeons passed. Another map shows a vast bulk of dry land around the south pole, where it is evident that some of the beings made experimental settlements, though their main centers were transferred to the nearest sea bottom. Later maps, which display the land mass as cracking and drifting, and sending certain detached parts northward, uphold in a striking way the theories of continental drift lately advanced by Taylor, Wegener, and Joly.

With the upheaval of new land in the South Pacific tremendous events began. Some of the marine cities were hopelessly shattered, yet that was not the worst misfortune. Another race—a land race of beings shaped like octopi and probably corresponding to fabulous pre-human spawn of Cthulhu—soon began filtering down from cosmic infinity and precipitated a monstrous war which for a time drove the Old Ones wholly back to the sea—a colossal blow in view of the increasing land settlements. Later, peace was made, and the new lands were given to the Cthulhu spawn whilst the Old Ones held the sea and the older lands. New land cities were founded—the greatest of them in the Antarctic, for this region of first arrival was sacred. From then on, as before, the Antarctic remained the center of the Old Ones' civilization, and all the cities built there by the Cthulhu spawn were blotted out. Then suddenly the lands of the Pacific sank again, taking with them the frightful stone city of R'lyeh and all the cosmic octopi, so that the Old Ones were again supreme on the planet except for one shadowy fear about which they did not like to speak. At a rather later age, their cities dotted all the land and water areas of the globe—hence, the recommendation in my coming monograph that some archaeologist make systematic borings with Pabodie's type of apparatus in certain widely separated regions.

The steady trend down the ages was from water to land—a movement encouraged by the rise of new land masses, though the ocean was never wholly deserted. Another cause of the landward movement was the new difficulty in breeding and managing the Shoggoths upon which successful sea life depended. With the march of time, as the sculptures sadly confessed, the art of creating new life from inorganic matter had been lost, so that the Old Ones had to depend on the molding of forms already in existence. On land, the great reptiles proved highly tractable; but the Shoggoths of the sea, reproducing by fission and acquiring a dangerous degree of accidental intelligence, presented for a time a formidable problem.

They had always been controlled through the hypnotic suggestions of the Old Ones, and had modeled their tough plasticity into various useful temporary limbs and organs; but now their self-modeling powers were sometimes exercised independently, and in various imitative forms implanted by past suggestion. They had, it seems, developed a semi-stable brain whose separate and occasionally stubborn volition echoed the will of the Old Ones without always obeying it. Sculptured images of these Shoggoths filled Danforth and me with horror and loathing. They were normally shapeless entities composed of a viscous jelly which looked like an agglutination of bubbles, and each averaged about fifteen feet in diameter when a sphere. They had, however, a constantly shifting shape and volume—throwing out temporary developments or forming apparent organs of sight, hearing, and speech in imitation of their masters, either spontaneously or according to suggestion.

They seem to have become peculiarly intractable toward the middle of the Permian Age, perhaps one hundred and fifty million years ago, when a veritable war of re-subjugation was waged upon them by the marine Old Ones. Pictures of this war, and of the headless, slime-coated fashion in which the Shoggoths typically left their slain victims, held a marvelously fearsome quality despite the intervening abyss of untold ages. The Old Ones had used curious weapons of molecular and atomic disturbances against the rebel entities, and in the end had achieved a complete victory. Thereafter the sculptures showed a period in which Shoggoths were tamed and broken by armed Old Ones as the wild horses of the American west were tamed by cowboys. Though during the rebellion, the Shoggoths had shown an ability to live out of water, this transition was not encouraged—since their usefulness on land would hardly have been commensurate with the trouble of their management.

During the Jurassic Age, the Old Ones met fresh adversity in the form of a new invasion from outer space—this time by half-fungous, half-crustacean creatures—creatures undoubtedly the same as those figuring in certain whispered hill legends of the north, and remembered in the Himalayas as the Mi-Go, or abominable snowmen. To fight these beings, the Old Ones attempted, for the first time since their terrene advent, to sally forth again into the planetary ether; but, despite all traditional preparations, found it no longer possible to leave the earth's atmosphere. Whatever the old secret of interstellar travel had been, it was now definitely lost to the race. In the end, the Mi-Go drove the Old Ones out of all the northern lands, though they were powerless to disturb those in the sea. Little by little the slow retreat of the elder race to their original Antarctic habitat was beginning.

It was curious to note from the pictured battles that both the Cthulhu spawn and the Mi-Go seem to have been composed of matter more widely different from that which we know than was the substance of the Old Ones. They were able to undergo transformations and re-integrations impossible for their adversaries, and seem therefore to have originally come from even remoter gulfs of the cosmic space. The Old Ones, but for their abnormal toughness and peculiar vital properties, were strictly material, and must have had their absolute origin within the known space-time continuum—whereas the first sources of the other beings can only be guessed at with bated breath. All this, of course, assuming that the non-terrestrial linkages and the anomalies ascribed to the invading foes are not pure mythology. Conceivably, the Old Ones might have invented a cosmic framework to account for their occasional defeats, since historical interest and pride obviously formed their chief psychological element. It is significant that their annals failed to mention many advanced and potent races of beings whose mighty cultures and towering cities figure persistently in certain obscure legends.

The changing state of the world through long geologic ages appeared with startling vividness in many of the sculptured maps and scenes. In certain cases, existing science will require revision, while in other cases, its bold deductions are magnificently confirmed. As I have said, the hypothesis of Taylor, Wegener, and Joly that all the continents are fragments of an original Antarctic land mass that cracked from centrifugal force and drifted apart over a technically viscous lower surface—a hypothesis suggested by such things as the complementary outlines of Africa and South America, and the way the great mountain chains are rolled and shoved up—receives striking support from this uncanny source.

Maps evidently showing the Carboniferous world of a hundred million or more years ago displayed significant rifts and chasms destined later to separate Africa from the once continuous realms of Europe (then the Valusia of primal legend), Asia, the Americas, and the Antarctic continent. Other charts—and most significantly one in connection with the founding fifty million years ago of the vast dead city around us—showed all the present continents well differentiated. And in the latest discoverable specimen, dating perhaps from the Pliocene Age, the approximate world of today appeared quite clearly despite the linkage of Alaska with Siberia, of North America with Europe through Greenland, and of South America with the Antarctic continent through Graham Land. In the Carboniferous map, the whole globe—ocean floor and rifted land mass alike—bore symbols of the Old Ones' vast stone cities; but in the later charts the gradual recession toward the Antarctic became very plain. The final Pliocene specimen showed no land cities except on the Antarctic continent and the tip of South America, nor any ocean cities north of the fiftieth parallel of South Latitude. Knowledge and interest in the northern world, save for a study of coastlines probably made during long exploration flights on those fan-like membranous wings, had evidently declined to zero among the Old Ones.

Destruction of cities through the upthrust of mountains, the centrifugal rending of continents, the seismic convulsions of land or sea-bottom, and other natural causes, was a matter of common record; and it was curious to observe how fewer and fewer replacements were made as the ages wore on. The vast dead megalopolis that yawned around us seemed to be the last general center of the race—built early in the Cretaceous Age after a titanic earth-buckling had obliterated a still vaster predecessor not far distant. It appeared that this general region was the most sacred spot of all, where reputedly the first Old Ones had settled on a primal sea-bottom. In the new city—many of whose features we could recognize in the sculptures, but which stretched fully a hundred miles along the mountain range in each direction beyond the farthest limits of our aerial survey—there were reputed to be preserved certain sacred stones forming part of the first sea-bottom city, which thrust up to light after long epochs in the course of the general crumpling of strata.

Chapter 8

Naturally, Danforth and I studied with especial interest and a peculiarly personal sense of awe everything pertaining to the immediate district in which we were. Of this local material there was naturally a vast abundance; and on the tangled ground level of the city we were lucky enough to find a house of very late date whose walls, though somewhat damaged by a neighboring rift, contained sculptures of decadent workmanship carrying the story of the region much beyond the period of the Pliocene map whence we derived our last general glimpse of the pre-human world. This was the last place we examined in detail, since what we found there gave us a fresh immediate objective.

Certainly, we were in one of the strangest, weirdest, and most terrible of all the corners of earth's globe. Of all existing lands, it was infinitely the most ancient. The conviction grew upon us that this hideous upland must indeed be the fabled nightmare plateau of Leng which even the mad author of the *Necronomicon* was reluctant to discuss. The great mountain chain was tremendously long—starting as a low range at Luitpold Land on the east coast of Weddell Sea and virtually crossing the entire continent. That really high part stretched in a mighty arc from about Latitude 82°, **e)** Longitude 60° to Latitude 70°, **e)** Longitude 115°, with its concave side toward our camp and its seaward end in the region of that long, ice-locked coast whose hills were glimpsed by Wilkes and Mawson at the Antarctic circle.

Yet even more monstrous exaggerations of nature seemed disturbingly close at hand. I have said that these peaks are higher than the Himalayas, but the sculptures forbid me to say that they are earth's highest. That grim honor is beyond doubt reserved for something which half the sculptures hesitated to record at all, whilst others approached it with obvious repugnance and trepidation. It seems that there was one part of the ancient land—the first part that ever rose from the waters after the earth had flung off the moon and the Old Ones had seeped down, from the stars—which had come to be shunned as vaguely and namelessly evil. Cities built there had crumbled before their time, and had been found suddenly deserted. Then when the first great earth buckling had convulsed the region in the Comanchian Age, a frightful line of peaks had shot suddenly up amidst the most appalling din and chaos—and earth had received her loftiest and most terrible mountains.

If the scale of the carvings was correct, these abhorred things must have been much over forty thousand feet high—radically vaster than even the shocking mountains of madness we had crossed. They extended, it appeared, from about Latitude 77°, **e)** Longitude 70° to Latitude 70°, **e)** Longitude 100°—less than three hundred miles away from the dead city, so that we would have spied their dreaded summits in the dim western distance had it not been for that vague, opalescent haze. Their northern end must likewise be visible from the long Antarctic circle coast line at Queen Mary Land.

Some of the Old Ones, in the decadent days, had made strange prayers to those mountains—but none ever went near them or dared to guess what lay beyond. No human eye had ever seen them, and as I studied the emotions conveyed in the carvings, I prayed that none ever might. There are protecting hills along the coast beyond them—Queen Mary and Kaiser Wilhelm Lands—and I thank Heaven no one has been able to land and climb those hills. I am not as skeptical about old tales and fears as I used to be, and I do not laugh now at the pre-human sculptor's notion that lightning paused meaningfully now and then at each of the brooding crests, and that an unexplained glow shone from one of those terrible pinnacles all through the long polar night. There may be a very real and very monstrous meaning in the old Pnakotic whispers about Kadath in the Cold Waste.

But the terrain close at hand was hardly less strange, even if less namelessly accursed. Soon after the founding of the city the great mountain range became the seat of the principal temples, and many carvings showed what grotesque and fantastic towers had pierced the sky where now we saw only the curiously clinging cubes and ramparts. In the course of ages, the caves had appeared, and had been shaped into adjuncts of the temples. With the advance of still later epochs, all the limestone veins of the region were hollowed out by ground waters, so that the mountains, the foothills, and the plains below them were a veritable network of connected caverns and galleries. Many graphic sculptures told of explorations deep underground, and of the final discovery of the Stygian sunless sea that lurked at earth's bowels.

This vast nighted gulf had undoubtedly been worn by the great river which flowed down from the nameless and horrible westward mountains, and which had formerly turned at the base of the Old Ones' range and flowed beside that chain into the Indian Ocean between Budd and Totten Lands on Wilkes's coast line. Little by little it had eaten away the limestone hill base at its turning, till at last its sapping currents reached the caverns of the ground waters and joined with them in digging a deeper abyss. Finally, its whole bulk emptied into the hollow hills and left the old bed toward the ocean dry. Much of the later city as we now found it had been built over that former bed. The Old Ones, understanding what had happened, and exercising their always keen artistic sense, had carved into ornate pylons those headlands of the foothills where the great stream began its descent into eternal darkness.

This river, once crossed by scores of noble stone bridges, was plainly the one whose extinct course we had seen in our aeroplane survey. Its position in different carvings of the city helped us to orient ourselves to the scene as it had been at various stages of the region's age-long, aeon-dead history, so that we were able to sketch a hasty but careful map of the salient features—squares, important buildings, and the like—for guidance in further explorations. We could soon reconstruct in fancy the whole stupendous thing as it was a million or ten million or fifty million years ago, for the sculptures told us exactly what the buildings and mountains and squares and suburbs and landscape setting and luxuriant Tertiary vegetation had looked like. It must have had a marvelous and mystic beauty, and as I thought of it, I almost forgot the clammy sense of sinister oppression with which the city's inhuman age and massiveness and deadness and remoteness and glacial twilight had choked and weighed on my spirit. Yet according to certain carvings, the denizens of that city had themselves known the clutch of oppressive terror; for there was a somber and recurrent type of scene in which the Old Ones were shown in the act of recoiling affrightedly from some object—never allowed to appear in the design—found in the great river and indicated as having been washed down through waving, vine-draped cycad forests from those horrible westward mountains.

It was only in the one late-built house with the decadent carvings that we obtained any foreshadowing of the final calamity leading to the city's desertion. Undoubtedly there must have been many sculptures of the same age elsewhere, even allowing for the slackened energies and aspirations of a stressful and uncertain period; indeed, very certain evidence of the existence of others came to us shortly afterward. But this was the first and only set we directly encountered. We meant to look farther later on; but as I have said, immediate conditions dictated another present objective. There would, though, have been a limit—for after all hope of a long future occupancy of the place had perished among the Old Ones, there could not but have been a complete cessation of mural decoration. The ultimate blow, of course, was the coming of the great cold which once held most of the earth in thrall, and which has never departed from the ill-fated poles—the great cold that, at the world's other extremity, put an end to the fabled lands of Lomar and Hyperborea.

Just when this tendency began in the Antarctic, it would be hard to say in terms of exact years. Nowadays we set the beginning of the general glacial periods at a distance of about five hundred thousand years from the present, but at the poles the terrible scourge must have commenced much earlier. All quantitative estimates are partly guesswork, but it is quite likely that the decadent sculptures were made considerably less than a million years ago, and that the actual desertion of the city was complete long before the conventional opening of the Pleistocene—five hundred thousand years ago—as reckoned in terms of the earth's whole surface.

In the decadent sculptures there were signs of thinner vegetation everywhere, and of a decreased country life on the part of the Old Ones. Heating devices were shown in the houses, and winter travelers were represented as muffled in protective fabrics. Then we saw a series of cartouches—the continuous band arrangement being frequently interrupted in these late carvings—depicting a constantly growing migration to the nearest refuges of greater warmth—some fleeing to cities under the sea off the far-away coast, and some clambering down through networks of limestone caverns in the hollow hills to the neighboring black abyss of subterrene waters.

In the end, it seems to have been the neighboring abyss that received the greatest colonization. This was partly due, no doubt, to the traditional sacredness of this special region, but may have been more conclusively determined by the opportunities it gave for continuing the use of the great temples on the honeycombed mountains, and for retaining the vast land city as a place of summer residence and base of communication with various mines. The linkage of old and new abodes was made more effective by means of several gradings and improvements along the connecting routes, including the chiseling of numerous direct tunnels from the ancient metropolis to the black abyss—sharply down-pointing tunnels whose mouths we carefully drew, according to our most thoughtful estimates, on the guide map we were compiling. It was obvious that at least two of these tunnels lay within a reasonable exploring distance of where we were—both being on the mountainward edge of the city, one less than a quarter of a mile toward the ancient river-course, and the other perhaps twice that distance in the opposite direction.

The abyss, it seems, had shelving shores of dry land at certain places, but the Old Ones built their new city under water—no doubt because of its greater certainty of uniform warmth. The depth of the hidden sea appears to have been very great, so that the earth's internal heat could ensure its habitability for an indefinite period. The beings seemed to have had no trouble in adapting themselves to part-time—and eventually, of course, whole-time—residence under water, since they had never allowed their gill systems to atrophy. There were many sculptures which showed how they had always frequently visited their submarine kinsfolk elsewhere, and how they had habitually bathed on the deep bottom of their great river. The darkness of inner earth could likewise have been no deterrent to a race accustomed to long Antarctic nights.

Decadent though their style undoubtedly was, these latest carvings had a truly epic quality where they told of the building of the new city in the cavern sea. The Old Ones had gone about it scientifically—quarrying insoluble rocks from the heart of the honeycombed mountains, and employing expert workers from the nearest submarine city to perform the construction according to the best methods. These workers brought with them all that was necessary to establish the new venture—Shoggoth tissue from which to breed stone lifters and subsequent beasts of burden for the cavern city, and other protoplasmic matter to mold into phosphorescent organisms for lighting purposes.

At last, a mighty metropolis rose on the bottom of that Stygian sea, its architecture much like that of the city above, and its workmanship displaying relatively little decadence because of the precise mathematical element inherent in building operations. The newly bred Shoggoths grew to enormous size and singular intelligence, and were represented as taking and executing orders with marvelous quickness. They seemed to converse with the Old Ones by mimicking their voices—a sort of musical piping over a wide range, if poor Lake's dissection had indicated aright—and to work more from spoken commands than from hypnotic suggestions as in earlier times. They were, however, kept in admirable control. The phosphorescent organisms supplied light with vast effectiveness, and doubtless atoned for the loss of the familiar polar auroras of the outer-world night.

Art and decoration were pursued, though of course with a certain decadence. The Old Ones seemed to realize this falling off themselves, and in many cases anticipated the policy of Constantine the Great by transplanting especially fine blocks of ancient carving from their land city, just as the emperor, in a similar age of decline, stripped Greece and Asia of their finest art to give his new Byzantine capital greater splendors than its own people could create. That the transfer of sculptured blocks had not been more extensive was doubtless owing to the fact that the land city was not at first wholly abandoned. By the time total abandonment did occur—and it surely must have occurred before the polar Pleistocene was far advanced—the Old Ones had perhaps become satisfied with their decadent art—or had ceased to recognize the superior merit of the older carvings. At any rate, the aeon-silent ruins around us had certainly undergone no wholesale sculptural denudation, though all the best separate statues, like other movables, had been taken away.

The decadent cartouches and dadoes telling this story were, as I have said, the latest we could find in our limited search. They left us with a picture of the Old Ones shuttling back and forth betwixt the land city in summer and the sea-cavern city in winter, and sometimes trading with the sea-bottom cities off the Antarctic coast. By this time the ultimate doom of the land city must have been recognized, for the sculptures showed many signs of the cold's malign encroachments. Vegetation was declining, and the terrible snows of the winter no longer melted completely even in midsummer. The saurian livestock were nearly all dead, and the mammals were standing it none too well. To keep on with the work of the upper world it had become necessary to adapt some of the amorphous and curiously cold-resistant Shoggoths to land life—a thing the Old Ones had formerly been reluctant to do. The great river was now lifeless, and the upper sea had lost most of its denizens except the seals and whales. All the birds had flown away, save only the great, grotesque penguins.

What had happened afterward we could only guess. How long had the new sea-cavern city survived? Was it still down there, a stony corpse in eternal blackness? Had the subterranean waters frozen at last? To what fate had the ocean-bottom cities of the outer world been delivered? Had any of the Old Ones shifted north ahead of the creeping ice cap? Existing geology shows no trace of their presence. Had the frightful Mi-Go been still a menace in the outer land world of the north? Could one be sure of what might or might not linger, even to this day, in the lightless and unplumbed abysses of earth's deepest waters? Those things had seemingly been able to withstand any amount of pressure—and men of the sea have fished up curious objects at times. And has the killer-whale theory really explained the savage and mysterious scars on Antarctic seals noticed a generation ago by Borchgrevingk?

The specimens found by poor Lake did not enter into these guesses, for their geologic setting proved them to have lived at what must have been a very early date in the land city's history. They were, according to their location, certainly not less than thirty million years old, and we reflected that in their day the sea-cavern city, and indeed the cavern itself, had had no existence. They would have remembered an older scene, with lush Tertiary vegetation everywhere, a younger land city of flourishing arts around them, and a great river sweeping northward along the base of the mighty mountains toward a far-away tropic ocean.

And yet we could not help thinking about these specimens—especially about the eight perfect ones that were missing from Lake's hideously ravaged camp. There was something abnormal about that whole business—the strange things we had tried so hard to lay to somebody's madness—those frightful graves—the amount *and nature* of the missing material—Gedney—the unearthly toughness of those archaic monstrosities, and the queer vital freaks the sculptures now showed the race to have—Danforth and I had seen a good deal in the last few hours, and were prepared to believe and keep silent about many appalling and incredible secrets of primal nature.

Chapter 9

I have said that our study of the decadent sculptures brought about a change in our immediate objective. This, of course, had to do with the chiseled avenues to the black inner world, of whose existence we had not known before but we were now eager to find and traverse. From the evident scale of the carvings we deduced that a steeply descending walk of about a mile through either of the neighboring tunnels would bring us to the brink of the dizzy, sunless cliffs above the great abyss, down whose sides paths, improved by the Old Ones, led to the rocky shore of the hidden and nighted ocean. To behold this fabulous gulf in stark reality was a lure which seemed impossible of resistance once we knew of the thing—yet we realized we must begin the quest at once if we expected to include it in our present trip.

It was now 8 p.m., and we did not have enough battery replacements to let our torches burn on forever. We had done so much studying and copying below the glacial level that our battery supply had had at least five hours of nearly continuous use, and despite the special dry cell formula, would obviously be good for only about four more—though by keeping one torch unused, except for especially interesting or difficult places, we might manage to eke out a safe margin beyond that. It would not do to be without a light in these Cyclopean catacombs; hence, to make the abyss trip, we must give up all further mural deciphering. Of course, we intended to revisit the place for days and perhaps weeks of intensive study and photography—curiosity having long ago got the better of horror—but just now we must hasten. Our supply of trail-blazing paper was far from unlimited, and we were reluctant to sacrifice spare notebooks or sketching paper to augment it, but we did let one large notebook go. If worse came to worst, we could resort to rock-chipping—and of course it would be possible, even in case of really lost direction, to work up to full daylight by one channel or another if granted sufficient time for plentiful trial and error. So at last we set off eagerly in the indicated direction of the nearest tunnel.

According to the carvings from which we had made our map, the desired tunnel-mouth could not be much more than a quarter of a mile from where we stood; the intervening space showing solid-looking buildings quite likely to be penetrable still at a sub-glacial level. The opening itself would be in the basement—on the angle nearest the foothills—of a vast five-pointed structure of evidently public and perhaps ceremonial nature, which we tried to identify from our aerial survey of the ruins. No such structure came to our minds as we recalled our flight, so we concluded that its upper parts had been greatly damaged, or that it had been totally shattered in an ice rift we had noticed. In the latter case, the tunnel would probably turn out to be choked, so we would have to try the next nearest one—the one less than a mile to the north. The intervening river course prevented our trying any of the more southern tunnels on this trip; and indeed, if both of the neighboring ones were choked, it was doubtful whether our batteries would warrant an attempt on the next northerly one—about a mile beyond our second choice.

As we threaded our dim way through the labyrinth with the aid of map and compass—traversing rooms and corridors in every stage of ruin or preservation, clambering up ramps, crossing upper floors and bridges and clambering down again, encountering choked doorways and piles of debris, hastening now and then along finely preserved and uncannily immaculate stretches, taking false leads and retracing our way (in such cases removing the blind paper trail we had left), and once in a while striking the bottom of an open shaft through which daylight poured or trickled down—we were repeatedly tantalized by the sculptured walls along our route. Many must have told tales of immense historical importance, and only the prospect of later visits reconciled us to the need of passing them by. As it was, we slowed down once in a while and turned on our second torch. If we had had more films, we would certainly have paused briefly to photograph certain bas-reliefs, but time-consuming hand-copying was clearly out of the question.

I come now once more to a place where the temptation to hesitate, or to hint rather than state, is very strong. It is necessary, however, to reveal the rest in order to justify my course in discouraging further exploration. We had wormed our way very close to the computed site of the tunnel's mouth—having crossed a second-story bridge to what seemed plainly the tip of a pointed wall, and descended to a ruinous corridor especially rich in decadently elaborate and apparently ritualistic sculptures of late workmanship—when, shortly before 8:30 p.m., Danforth's keen young nostrils gave us the first hint of something unusual. If we'd had a dog with us, I suppose we would have been warned before. At first, we could not precisely say what was wrong with the formerly crystal-pure air, but after a few seconds, our memories reacted only too definitely. Let me try to state the thing without flinching. There was an odor—and that odor was vaguely, subtly, and unmistakably akin to what had nauseated us upon opening the insane grave of the horror poor Lake had dissected.

Of course, the revelation was not as clearly cut at the time as it sounds now. There were several conceivable explanations, and we did a good deal of indecisive whispering. Most important of all, we did not retreat without further investigation; for having come this far, we were loath to be balked by anything short of certain disaster. Anyway, what we must have suspected was altogether too wild to believe. Such things did not happen in any normal world. It was probably sheer irrational instinct which made us dim our single torch—tempted no longer by the decadent and sinister sculptures that leered menacingly from the oppressive walls—and which softened our progress to a cautious tiptoeing and crawling over the increasingly littered floor and heaps of debris.

Danforth's eyes as well as nose proved better than mine, for it was likewise he who first noticed the queer aspect of the debris after we had passed many half-choked arches leading to chambers and corridors on the ground level. It did not look quite as it ought after countless thousands of years of desertion, and when we cautiously turned on more light, we saw that a kind of swath seemed to have been lately tracked through it. The irregular nature of the litter precluded any definite marks, but in the smoother places there were suggestions of the dragging of heavy objects. Once we thought there was a hint of parallel tracks as if of runners. This was what made us pause again.

It was during that pause that we caught—simultaneously this time—the other odor ahead. Paradoxically, it was both a less frightful and more frightful odor—less frightful intrinsically, but infinitely appalling in this place under the known circumstances—unless, of course, Gedney—for the odor was the plain and familiar one of common petrol—everyday gasoline.

Our motivation after that is something I will leave to psychologists. We knew now that some terrible extension of the camp horrors must have crawled into this nighted burial place of the aeons, hence, we could not doubt any longer the existence of nameless conditions—present or at least recent—just ahead. Yet, in the end, we did let sheer burning curiosity—or anxiety—or autohypnotism—or vague thoughts of responsibility toward Gedney—or what not—drive us on. Danforth whispered again of the print he thought he had seen at the alley-turning in the ruins above; and of the faint musical piping—potentially of tremendous significance in the light of Lake's dissection report, despite its close resemblance to the cave-mouth echoes of the windy peaks—which he thought he had shortly afterward half heard from unknown depths below. I, in my turn, whispered of how the camp was left—of what had disappeared, and of how the madness of a lone survivor might have conceived the inconceivable—a wild trip across the monstrous mountains and a descent into the unknown, primal masonry—But we could not convince each other, or even ourselves, of anything definite. We had turned off all light as we stood still, and vaguely noticed that a trace of deeply filtered upper day kept the blackness from being absolute. Having automatically begun to move ahead, we guided ourselves by occasional flashes from our torch. The disturbed debris formed an impression we could not shake off, and the smell of gasoline grew stronger. More and more ruin met our eyes and hampered our feet, until very soon we saw that the forward way was about to cease. We had been all too correct in our pessimistic guess about that rift glimpsed from the air. Our tunnel quest was a blind one, and we were not even going to be able to reach the basement out of which the abyssward aperture opened.

The torch, flashing over the grotesquely carved walls of the blocked corridor in which we stood, showed several doorways in various states of obstruction; and from one of them the gasoline odor—quite submerging that other hint of odor—came with especial distinctness. As we looked more steadily, we saw that beyond a doubt there had been a slight and recent clearing away of debris from that particular opening. Whatever the lurking horror might be, we believed the direct avenue toward it was now plainly manifest. I do not think anyone will wonder that we waited an appreciable time before making any further motion.

And yet, when we did venture inside that black arch, our first impression was one of anticlimax. For amidst the littered expanse of that sculptured Crypt—a perfect cube with sides of about twenty feet—there remained no recent object of instantly discernible size; so that we looked instinctively, though in vain, for a farther doorway. In another moment, however, Danforth's sharp vision had descried a place where the floor debris had been disturbed; and we turned on both torches full strength. Though what we saw in that light was actually simple and trifling, I am nonetheless reluctant to tell of it because of what it implied. It was a rough leveling of the debris, upon which several small objects lay carelessly scattered, and at one corner of which a considerable amount of gasoline must have been spilled lately enough to leave a strong odor even at this extreme super-plateau altitude. In other words, it could not be other than a sort of camp—a camp made by questing beings who, like us, had been turned back by the unexpectedly choked way to the abyss.

Let me be plain. The scattered objects were, so far as substance was concerned, all from Lake's camp; and consisted of tin cans as queerly opened as those we had seen at that ravaged place; many spent matches; three illustrated books more or less curiously smudged; an empty ink bottle with its pictorial and instructional carton; a broken fountain pen; some oddly snipped fragments of fur and tent-cloth; a used electric battery with circular of directions; a folder that came with our type of tent heater; and a sprinkling of crumpled papers. It was all bad enough, but when we smoothed out the papers and looked at what was on them, we felt we had come to the worst. We had found certain inexplicably blotted papers at the camp which might have prepared us, yet the effect of the sight down there in the pre-human vaults of a nightmare city was almost too much to bear.

A mad Gedney might have made the groups of dots in imitation of those found on the greenish soapstones, just as the dots on those insane five-pointed grave-mounds might have been made; and he might conceivably have prepared rough, hasty sketches—varying in their accuracy or lack of it—which outlined the neighboring parts of the city and traced the way from a circularly represented place outside our previous route—a place we identified as a great cylindrical tower in the carvings and as a vast circular gulf glimpsed in our aerial survey—to the present five-pointed structure and the tunnel-mouth therein. He might, I repeat, have prepared such sketches; for those before us were quite obviously compiled, as our own had been, from late sculptures somewhere in the glacial labyrinth, though not from the ones which we had seen and used. But what that art-blind bungler could never have done was to execute those sketches in a strange and assured technique perhaps superior, despite haste and carelessness, to any of the decadent carvings from which they were taken—the characteristic and unmistakable technique of the Old Ones themselves in the dead city's heyday.

There are those who will say Danforth and I were utterly mad not to flee for our lives after that; since our conclusions were now—notwithstanding their wildness—completely fixed, and of a nature I need not even mention to those who have read my account as far as this. Perhaps we were mad—for have I not said those horrible peaks were mountains of madness? But I think I can detect something of the same spirit—albeit in a less extreme form—in the men who stalk deadly beasts through African jungles to photograph them or study their habits. Half-paralyzed with terror though we were, there was nevertheless fanned within us a blazing flame of awe and curiosity that triumphed in the end.

Of course, we did not mean to face that—or those—which we knew had been there, but we felt that they must be gone by now. They would by this time have found the other neighboring entrance to the abyss, and have passed within, to whatever night-black fragments of the past might await them in the ultimate gulf—the ultimate gulf they had never seen. Or if that entrance too was blocked, they would have gone on to the north seeking another. They were, we remembered, partly independent of light.

Looking back to that moment, I can scarcely recall what precise form our new emotions took—just what change of immediate objective it was that so sharpened our sense of expectancy. We certainly did not mean to face what we feared—yet I will not deny that we may have had a lurking, unconscious wish to spy certain things from some hidden vantage point. Probably we had not given up our zeal to glimpse the abyss itself, though there was interposed a new goal in the form of that great circular place shown on the crumpled sketches we had found. We had at once recognized it as a monstrous cylindrical tower figuring in the very earliest carvings, but appearing only as a prodigious round aperture from above. Something about the impressiveness of its rendering, even in these hasty diagrams, made us think that its subglacial levels must still form a feature of peculiar importance. Perhaps it embodied architectural marvels as yet unencountered by us. It was certainly of incredible age according to the sculptures in which it figured—being indeed among the first things built in the city. Its carvings, if preserved, could not but be highly significant. Moreover, it might form a good present link with the upper world—a shorter route than the one we were so carefully blazing, and probably that by which those others had descended.

At any rate, the thing we did was to study the terrible sketches—which quite perfectly confirmed our own—and start back over the indicated course to the circular place; the course which our nameless predecessors must have traversed twice before us. The other neighboring gate to the abyss would lie beyond that. I need not speak of our journey—during which we continued to leave an economical trail of paper—for it was precisely the same in kind as that by which we had reached the cul-de-sac; except that it tended to adhere more closely to the ground level and even descend to basement corridors. Every now and then, we could trace certain disturbing marks in the debris or litter underfoot; and after we had passed outside the radius of the gasoline scent, we were again faintly conscious—spasmodically—of that more hideous and more persistent scent. After the way had branched from our former course, we sometimes gave the rays of our single torch a furtive sweep along the walls; noting in almost every case the well-nigh omnipresent sculptures, which indeed seem to have formed a main aesthetic outlet for the Old Ones.

About 9:30 p.m., while traversing a long, vaulted corridor whose increasingly glaciated floor seemed somewhat below the ground level and whose roof grew lower as we advanced, we began to see strong daylight ahead and were able to turn off our torch. It appeared that we were coming to the vast circular place, and that our distance from the upper air could not be very great. The corridor ended in an arch surprisingly low for these megalithic ruins, but we could see much through it even before we emerged. Beyond there stretched a prodigious round space—fully two hundred feet in diameter—strewn with debris and containing many choked archways corresponding to the one we were about to cross. The walls were—in available spaces—boldly sculptured into a spiral band of heroic proportions; and displayed, despite the destructive weathering caused by the openness of the spot, an artistic splendor far beyond anything we had encountered before. The littered floor was quite heavily glaciated, and we fancied that the true bottom lay at a considerably lower depth.

But the salient object of the place was the titanic stone ramp which, eluding the archways by a sharp turn outward into the open floor, wound spirally up the stupendous cylindrical wall like an inside counterpart of those once climbing outside the monstrous towers or ziggurats of antique Babylon. Only the rapidity of our flight, and the perspective which confounded the descent with the tower's inner wall, had prevented our noticing this feature from the air, and thus caused us to seek another avenue to the sub-glacial level. Pabodie might have been able to tell what sort of engineering held it in place, but Danforth and I could merely admire and marvel. We could see mighty stone corbels and pillars here and there, but what we saw seemed inadequate to the function performed. The thing was excellently preserved up to the present top of the tower—a highly remarkable circumstance in view of its exposure—and its shelter had done much to protect the bizarre and disturbing cosmic sculptures on the walls.

As we stepped out into the awesome half-daylight of this monstrous cylinder-bottom—fifty million years old, and without doubt the most primally ancient structure ever to meet our eyes—we saw that the ramp-traversed sides stretched dizzily up to a height of fully sixty feet. This, we recalled from our aerial survey, meant an outside glaciation of some forty feet; since the yawning gulf we had seen from the plane had been at the top of an approximately twenty-foot mound of crumbled masonry, somewhat sheltered for three-fourths of its circumference by the massive curving walls of a line of higher ruins. According to the sculptures, the original tower had stood in the center of an immense circular plaza, and had been perhaps five hundred or six hundred feet high, with tiers of horizontal disks near the top, and a row of needle-like spires along the upper rim. Most of the masonry had obviously toppled outward rather than inward—a fortunate happening, since otherwise the ramp might have been shattered and the whole interior choked. As it was, the ramp showed sad battering; whilst the choking was such that all the archways at the bottom seemed to have been recently cleared.

It took us only a moment to conclude that this was indeed the route by which those others had descended, and that this would be the logical route for our own ascent despite the long trail of paper we had left elsewhere. The tower's mouth was no farther from the foothills and our waiting plane than was the great terraced building we had entered, and any further sub-glacial exploration we might make on this trip would lie in this general region. Oddly, we were still thinking about possible later trips—even after all we had seen and guessed. Then, as we picked our way cautiously over the debris of the great floor, there came a sight which for the time excluded all other matters.

It was the neatly huddled array of three sledges in that farther angle of the ramp's lower and outward-projecting course which had hitherto been screened from our view. There they were—the three sledges missing from Lake's camp—shaken by a hard usage which must have included forcible dragging along great reaches of snowless masonry and debris, as well as much hand portage over utterly unnavigable places. They were carefully and intelligently packed and strapped, and contained things memorably familiar enough: the gasoline stove, fuel cans, instrument cases, provision tins, tarpaulins obviously bulging with books, and some bulging with less obvious contents—everything derived from Lake's equipment.

After what we had found in that other room, we were in a measure prepared for this encounter. The really great shock came when we stepped over and undid one tarpaulin whose outlines had peculiarly disquieted us. It seems that others as well as Lake had been interested in collecting typical specimens; for there were two here, both stiffly frozen, perfectly preserved, patched with adhesive plaster where some wounds around the neck had occurred, and wrapped with care to prevent further damage. They were the bodies of young Gedney and the missing dog.

Chapter 10

Many people will probably judge us callous as well as mad for thinking about the northward tunnel and the abyss so soon after our somber discovery, and I am not prepared to say that we would have immediately revived such thoughts but for a specific circumstance which broke in upon us and set up a whole new train of speculations. We had replaced the tarpaulin over poor Gedney and were standing in a kind of mute bewilderment when the sounds finally reached our consciousness—the first sounds we had heard since descending out of the open where the mountain wind whined faintly from its unearthly heights. Well known and mundane though they were, their presence in this remote world of death was more unexpected and unnerving than any grotesque or fabulous tones could possibly have been—since they gave a fresh upsetting to all our notions of cosmic harmony.

Had it been some trace of that bizarre musical piping over a wide range which Lake's dissection report had led us to expect in those others—and which, indeed, our overwrought fancies had been reading into every wind howl we had heard since coming on the camp horror—it would have had a kind of hellish congruity with the aeon-dead region around us. A voice from other epochs belongs in a graveyard of other epochs. As it was, however, the noise shattered all our profoundly seated adjustments—all our tacit acceptance of the inner Antarctic as a waste utterly and irrevocably void of every vestige of normal life. What we heard was not the fabulous note of any buried blasphemy of elder earth from whose supernal toughness an age-denied polar sun had evoked a monstrous response. Instead, it was a thing so mockingly normal and so unerringly familiarized by our sea days off Victoria Land and our camp days at McMurdo Sound that we shuddered to think of it here, where such things ought not to be. To be brief—it was simply the raucous squawking of a penguin.

The muffled sound floated from sub-glacial recesses nearly opposite to the corridor whence we had come—regions manifestly in the direction of that other tunnel to the vast abyss. The presence of a living water-bird in such a direction—in a world whose surface was one of age-long and uniform lifelessness—could lead to only one conclusion; hence, our first thought was to verify the objective reality of the sound. It was, indeed, repeated, and seemed at times to come from more than one throat. Seeking its source, we entered an archway from which much debris had been cleared; resuming our trail-blazing—with an added paper-supply taken with curious repugnance from one of the tarpaulin bundles on the sledges—when we left daylight behind.

As the glaciated floor gave place to a litter of detritus, we plainly discerned some curious, dragging tracks; and once Danforth found a distinct print of a sort whose description would be only too superfluous. The course indicated by the penguin cries was precisely what our map and compass prescribed as an approach to the more northerly tunnel-mouth, and we were glad to find that a bridgeless thoroughfare on the ground and basement levels seemed open. The tunnel, according to the chart, ought to start from the basement of a large pyramidal structure which we seemed vaguely to recall from our aerial survey as remarkably well-preserved. Along our path the single torch showed a customary profusion of carvings, but we did not pause to examine any of these.

Suddenly, a bulky white shape loomed up ahead of us, and we flashed on the second torch. It is odd how wholly this new quest had turned our minds from earlier fears of what might lurk near. Those other ones, having left their supplies in the great circular place, must have planned to return after their scouting trip toward or into the abyss; yet we had now discarded all caution concerning them as completely as if they had never existed. This white, waddling thing was fully six feet high, yet we seemed to realize at once that it was not one of those others. They were larger and dark, and, according to the sculptures, their motion over land surfaces was a swift, assured matter despite the queerness of their sea-born tentacle equipment. But to say that the white thing did not profoundly frighten us would be vain. We were indeed clutched for an instant by a primitive dread almost sharper than the worst of our reasoned fears regarding those others. Then came a flash of anticlimax as the white shape sidled into a lateral archway to our left to join two others of its kind which had summoned it in raucous tones. For it was only a penguin—albeit of a huge, unknown species larger than the greatest of the known king penguins, and monstrous in its combined albinism and virtual eyelessness.

When we had followed the thing into the archway and turned both our torches on the indifferent and unheeding group of three, we saw that they were all eyeless albinos of the same unknown and gigantic species. Their size reminded us of some of the archaic penguins depicted in the Old Ones' sculptures, and it did not take us long to conclude that they were descended from the same stock—undoubtedly surviving through a retreat to some warmer inner region whose perpetual blackness had destroyed their pigmentation and atrophied their eyes to mere useless slits. That their present habitat was the vast abyss we sought was not for a moment to be doubted; and this evidence of the gulf's continued warmth and habitability filled us with the most curious and subtly perturbing fancies.

We wondered, too, what had caused these three birds to venture out of their usual domain. The state and silence of the great dead city made it clear that it had at no time been a habitual seasonal rookery, whilst the manifest indifference of the trio to our presence made it seem odd that any passing party of those others should have startled them. Was it possible that those others had taken some aggressive action or tried to increase their meat supply? We doubted whether that pungent odor that the dogs had hated could cause an equal antipathy in these penguins, since their ancestors had obviously lived on excellent terms with the Old Ones—an amicable relationship which must have survived in the abyss below as long as any of the Old Ones remained. Regretting—in a flare-up of the old spirit of pure science—that we could not photograph these anomalous creatures, we shortly left them to their squawking and pushed on toward the abyss whose openness was now so positively proved to us, and whose exact direction occasional penguin tracks made clear.

Not long afterward, a steep descent in a long, low, doorless, and oddly sculptureless corridor led us to believe that we were approaching the tunnel-mouth at last. We had passed two more penguins and heard others immediately ahead. Then the corridor ended in a prodigious open space which made us gasp involuntarily—a perfect inverted hemisphere, obviously deep underground; fully a hundred feet in diameter and fifty feet high, with low archways opening around all parts of the circumference but one, and that one yawning cavernously with a black, arched aperture which broke the symmetry of the vault to a height of nearly fifteen feet. It was the entrance to the great abyss.

In this vast hemisphere, whose concave roof was impressively though decadently carved to a likeness of the primordial celestial dome, a few albino penguins waddled—aliens there, but indifferent and unseeing. The black tunnel yawned indefinitely off at a steep, descending grade, its aperture adorned with grotesquely chiseled jambs and lintel. From that cryptical mouth we fancied a current of slightly warmer air, and perhaps even a suspicion of vapor proceeded; and we wondered what living entities other than penguins the limitless void below, and the contiguous honeycombings of the land and the titan mountains, might conceal. We wondered, too, whether the trace of mountaintop smoke at first suspected by poor Lake, as well as the odd haze we had ourselves perceived around the rampart-crowned peak, might not be caused by the tortuous-channeled rising of some such vapor from the unfathomed regions of earth's core.

Entering the tunnel, we saw that its outline was—at least at the start—about fifteen feet each way—sides, floor, and arched roof composed of the usual megalithic masonry. The sides were sparsely decorated with cartouches of conventional designs in a late, decadent style; and all the construction and carving were marvelously well-preserved. The floor was quite clear, except for a slight detritus bearing outgoing penguin tracks and the inward tracks of these others. The farther one advanced, the warmer it became; so that we were soon unbuttoning our heavy garments. We wondered whether there were any actually igneous manifestations below, and whether the waters of that sunless sea were hot. After a short distance the masonry gave place to solid rock, though the tunnel kept the same proportions and presented the same aspect of carved regularity. Occasionally its varying grade became so steep that grooves were cut in the floor. Several times we noted the mouths of small lateral galleries not recorded in our diagrams; none of them such as to complicate the problem of our return, and all of them welcome as possible refuges in case we met unwelcome entities on their way back from the abyss. The nameless scent of such things was very distinct. Doubtless it was suicidally foolish to venture into that tunnel under the known conditions, but the lure of the unplumbed is stronger in certain persons than most suspect—indeed, it was just such a lure which had brought us to this unearthly polar waste in the first place. We saw several penguins as we passed along, and speculated on the distance we would have to traverse. The carvings had led us to expect a steep downhill walk of about a mile to the abyss, but our previous wanderings had shown us that matters of scale were not wholly to be depended on.

After about a quarter of a mile that nameless scent became greatly accentuated, and we kept very careful track of the various lateral openings we passed. There was no visible vapor as at the mouth, but this was doubtless due to the lack of contrasting cooler air. The temperature was rapidly ascending, and we were not surprised to come upon a careless heap of material shudderingly familiar to us. It was composed of furs and tent-cloth taken from Lake's camp, and we did not pause to study the bizarre forms into which the fabrics had been slashed. Slightly beyond this point, we noticed a decided increase in the size and number of the side galleries and concluded that the densely honeycombed region beneath the higher foothills must now have been reached. The nameless scent was now curiously mixed with another and scarcely less offensive odor—of what nature we could not guess, though we thought of decaying organisms and perhaps unknown subterranean fungi. Then came a startling expansion of the tunnel for which the carvings had not prepared us—a broadening and rising into a lofty, natural-looking elliptical cavern with a level floor, some seventy-five feet long and fifty broad and with many immense side passages leading away into cryptical darkness.

Though this cavern was natural in appearance, an inspection with both torches suggested that it had been formed by the artificial destruction of several walls between adjacent honeycombings. The walls were rough, and the high, vaulted roof was thick with stalactites; but the solid rock floor had been smoothed off and was free from all debris, detritus, or even dust to a positively abnormal extent. Except for the avenue through which we had come, this was true of the floors of all the great galleries opening off from it; and the singularity of the condition was such as to set us vainly puzzling. The curious new fetor which had supplemented the nameless scent was excessively pungent here; so much so that it destroyed all trace of the other. Something about this whole place, with its polished and almost glistening floor, struck us as more vaguely baffling and horrible than any of the monstrous things we had previously encountered.

The regularity of the passage immediately ahead, as well as the larger proportion of penguin-droppings there, prevented all confusion as to the right course amidst this plethora of equally great cave mouths. Nevertheless, we resolved to resume our paper trailblazing if any further complexity should develop; for dust tracks, of course, could no longer be expected. Upon resuming our direct progress, we cast a beam of torchlight over the tunnel walls—and stopped short in amazement at the supremely radical change which had come over the carvings in this part of the passage. We realized, of course, the great decadence of the Old Ones' sculpture at the time of the tunneling, and had indeed noticed the inferior workmanship of the arabesques in the stretches behind us. But now, in this deeper section beyond the cavern, there was a sudden difference wholly transcending explanation—a difference in basic nature as well as in mere quality, and involving so profound and calamitous a degradation of skill that nothing in the hitherto observed rate of decline could have led one to expect it.

This new and degenerate work was coarse, bold, and wholly lacking in delicacy of detail. It was countersunk with exaggerated depth in bands following the same general line as the sparse cartouches of the earlier sections, but the height of the reliefs did not reach the level of the general surface. Danforth had the idea that it was a second carving—a sort of palimpsest formed after the obliteration of a previous design. In nature it was wholly decorative and conventional, and consisted of crude spirals and angles roughly following the quintile mathematical tradition of the Old Ones, yet seemingly more like a parody than a perpetuation of that tradition. We could not get it out of our minds that some subtly but profoundly alien element had been added to the aesthetic feeling behind the technique—an alien element, Danforth guessed, that was responsible for the laborious substitution. It was like, yet disturbingly unlike, what we had come to recognize as the Old Ones' art; and I was persistently reminded of such hybrid things as the ungainly Palmyrene sculptures fashioned in the Roman manner. That others had recently noticed this belt of carving was hinted by the presence of a used flashlight battery on the floor in front of one of the most characteristic cartouches.

Since we could not afford to spend any considerable time in study, we resumed our advance after a cursory look; though frequently casting beams over the walls to see if any further decorative changes developed. Nothing of the sort was perceived, though the carvings were in places rather sparse because of the numerous mouths of smooth-floored lateral tunnels. We saw and heard fewer penguins, but thought we caught a vague suspicion of an infinitely distant chorus of them somewhere deep within the earth. The new and inexplicable odor was abominably strong, and we could detect scarcely a sign of that other nameless scent. Puffs of visible vapor ahead bespoke increasing contrasts in temperature, and the relative nearness of the sunless sea-cliffs of the great abyss. Then, quite unexpectedly, we saw certain obstructions on the polished floor ahead—obstructions which were quite definitely not penguins—and we turned on our second torch after making sure that the objects were quite stationary.

Chapter 11

Still another time have I come to a place where it is very difficult to proceed. I ought to be hardened by this stage; but there are some experiences and intimations which scar too deeply to permit healing, and leave only such an added sensitiveness that memory re-inspires all the original horror. We saw, as I have said, certain obstructions on the polished floor ahead; and I may add that our nostrils were assailed almost simultaneously by a very curious intensification of the strange prevailing fetor, now quite plainly mixed with the nameless stench of those others which had gone before. The light of the second torch left no doubt of what the obstructions were, and we dared approach them only because we could see, even from a distance, that they were quite as past all harming power as had been the six similar specimens unearthed from the monstrous star-mounded graves at poor Lake's camp.

They were, indeed, as lacking in completeness as most of those we had unearthed—though it grew plain from the thick, dark-green pool gathering around them that their incompleteness was of infinitely greater recency. There seemed to be only four of them, whereas Lake's bulletins would have suggested no less than eight as forming the group which had preceded us. To find them in this state was wholly unexpected, and we wondered what sort of monstrous struggle had occurred down here in the dark.

Penguins, attacked in a body, retaliate savagely with their beaks, and our ears now made certain the existence of a rookery far beyond. Had those others disturbed such a place and aroused murderous pursuit? The obstructions did not suggest it, for penguins' beaks against the tough tissues Lake had dissected could hardly account for the terrible damage our approaching glance was beginning to make out. Besides, the huge blind birds we had seen appeared to be singularly peaceful.

Had there, then, been a struggle among those others, and were the absent four responsible? If so, where were they? Were they close at hand and likely to form an immediate menace to us? We glanced anxiously at some of the smooth-floored lateral passages as we continued our slow and frankly reluctant approach. Whatever the conflict was, it had clearly been that which had frightened the penguins into their unaccustomed wandering. It must, then, have arisen near that faintly heard rookery in the incalculable gulf beyond, since there were no signs that any birds had normally dwelt here. Perhaps, we reflected, there had been a hideous running fight, with the weaker party seeking to get back to the cached sledges when their pursuers finished them. One could picture the demoniac fray between namelessly monstrous entities as it surged out of the black abyss with great clouds of frantic penguins squawking and scurrying ahcad.

I say that we approached those sprawling and incomplete obstructions slowly and reluctantly. Would to Heaven we had never approached them at all, but had run back at top speed out of that blasphemous tunnel with the greasily smooth floors and the degenerate murals aping and mocking the things they had superseded—run back, before we had seen what we did see, and before our minds were burned with something which will never let us breathe easily again!

Both of our torches were turned on the prostrate objects, so that we soon realized the dominant factor in their incompleteness. Mauled, compressed, twisted, and ruptured as they were, their chief common injury was total decapitation. From each one the tentacled starfish-head had been removed; and as we drew near, we saw that the manner of removal looked more like some hellish tearing or suction than like any ordinary form of cleavage. Their noisome dark-green ichor formed a large, spreading pool; but its stench was half overshadowed by the newer and stranger stench, here more pungent than at any other point along our route. Only when we had come very close to the sprawling obstructions could we trace that second, unexplainable fetor to any immediate source—and the instant we did so Danforth, remembering certain very vivid sculptures of the Old Ones' history in the Permian Age one hundred and fifty million years ago, gave vent to a nerve-tortured cry which echoed hysterically through that vaulted and archaic passage with the evil, palimpsest carvings.

I came only just short of echoing his cry myself; for I had seen those primal sculptures too, and had shudderingly admired the way the nameless artist had suggested that hideous slime coating found on certain incomplete and prostrate Old Ones—those whom the frightful Shoggoths had characteristically slain and sucked to a ghastly headlessness in the great war of re-subjugation. They were infamous, nightmare sculptures even when telling of age-old, bygone things; for Shoggoths and their work ought not to be seen by human beings or portrayed by any beings. The mad author of the *Necronomicon* had nervously tried to swear that none had been bred on this planet, and that only drugged dreamers had even conceived them. Formless protoplasm able to mock and reflect all forms and organs and processes—viscous agglutinations of bubbling cells—rubbery fifteen-foot spheroids infinitely plastic and ductile—slaves of suggestion, builders of cities—more and more sullen, more and more intelligent, more and more amphibious, more and more imitative! Great God! What madness made even those blasphemous Old Ones willing to use and carve such things?

And now, when Danforth and I saw the freshly glistening and reflectively iridescent black slime which clung thickly to those headless bodies and stank obscenely with that new, unknown odor whose cause only a diseased fancy could envisage—clung to those bodies and sparkled less voluminously on a smooth part of the accursedly resculptured wall in a series of grouped dots—we understood the quality of cosmic fear to its uttermost depths. It was not fear of those four missing others—for all too well did we suspect they would do no harm again. Poor devils! After all, they were not evil things of their kind. They were the men of another age and another order of being. Nature had played a hellish jest on them—as it will on any others that human madness, callousness, or cruelty may hereafter dig up in that hideously dead or sleeping polar waste—and this was their tragic homecoming. They had not been even savages—for what indeed had they done? That awful awakening in the cold of an unknown epoch—perhaps an attack by the furry, frantically barking quadrupeds, and a dazed defense against them and the equally frantic white simians with the queer wrappings and paraphernalia. . .poor Lake, poor Gedney. . .and poor Old Ones! Scientists to the last—what had they done that we would not have done in their place? God, what intelligence and persistence! What a facing of the incredible, just as those carven kinsmen and forbears had faced things only a bit less incredible! Radiates, vegetables, monstrosities, star-spawn —whatever they had been, they were men!

They had crossed the icy peaks on whose templed slopes they had once worshipped and roamed among the tree-ferns. They had found their dead city brooding under its curse, and had read its carven latter days as we had done. They had tried to reach their living fellows in fabled depths of blackness they had never seen—and what had they found? All this flashed in unison through the thoughts of Danforth and me as we looked from those headless, slime-coated shapes to the loathsome palimpsest sculptures and the diabolical dot-groups of fresh slime on the wall beside them—looked and understood what must have triumphed and survived down there in the Cyclopean water-city of that nighted, penguin-fringed abyss, whence even now a sinister curling mist had begun to belch pallidly as if in answer to Danforth's hysterical scream.

The shock of recognizing that monstrous slime and headlessness had frozen us into mute, motionless statues, and it is only through later conversations that we have learned of the complete identity of our thoughts at that moment. It seemed aeons that we stood there, but actually it could not have been more than ten or fifteen seconds. That hateful, pallid mist curled forward as if veritably driven by some remoter advancing bulk—and then came a sound which upset much of what we had just decided, and in so doing broke the spell and enabled us to run like mad past squawking, confused penguins over our former trail back to the city, along ice-sunken megalithic corridors to the great open circle, and up that archaic spiral ramp in a frenzied, automatic plunge for the sane outer air and light of day.

The new sound, as I have intimated, upset much that we had decided; because it was what poor Lake's dissection had led us to attribute to those we had judged dead. It was, Danforth later told me, precisely what he had caught in infinitely muffled form when at that spot beyond the alley corner above the glacial level; and it certainly had a shocking resemblance to the wind-pipings we had both heard around the lofty mountain caves. At the risk of seeming puerile I will add another thing, too, if only because of the surprising way Danforth's impressions chimed with mine. Of course, common reading is what prepared us both to make the interpretation, though Danforth has hinted at queer notions about unsuspected and forbidden sources to which Poe may have had access when writing his *Arthur Gordon Pym* a century ago. It will be remembered that in that fantastic tale there is a word of unknown but terrible and prodigious significance connected with the Antarctic and screamed eternally by the gigantic spectrally snowy birds of that malign region's core. *"Tekeli-li! Tekeli-li!"* That, I may admit, is exactly what we thought we heard conveyed by that sudden sound behind the advancing white mist—that insidious musical piping over a singularly wide range.

We were in full flight before three notes or syllables had been uttered, though we knew that the swiftness of the Old Ones would enable any scream-roused and pursuing survivor of the slaughter to overtake us in a moment if it really wished to do so. We had a vague hope, however, that non-aggressive conduct and a display of kindred reason might cause such a being to spare us in case of capture, if only from scientific curiosity. After all, if such an one had nothing to fear for itself, it would have no motive in harming us. Concealment being futile at this juncture, we used our torch for a running glance behind, and perceived that the mist was thinning. Would we see, at last, a complete and living specimen of those others? Again came that insidious musical piping—*"Tekeli-li! Tekeli-li!"* Then, noting that we were actually gaining on our pursuer, it occurred to us that the entity might be wounded. We could take no chances, however, since it was very obviously approaching in answer to Danforth's scream, rather than in flight from any other entity. The timing was too close to admit of doubt. Of the whereabouts of that less conceivable and less mentionable nightmare—that fetid, unglimpsed mountain of slime-spewing protoplasm whose race had conquered the abyss and sent land pioneers to re-carve and squirm through the burrows of the hills—we could form no guess; and it cost us a genuine pang to leave this probably crippled Old One—perhaps a lone survivor—to the peril of recapture and a nameless fate.

Thank Heaven we did not slacken our run. The curling mist had thickened again and was driving ahead with increased speed; whilst the straying penguins in our rear were squawking and screaming and displaying signs of a panic really surprising in view of their relatively minor confusion when we had passed them. Once more came that sinister, wide-ranged piping—*"Tekeli-li! Tekeli-li!"* We had been wrong. The thing was not wounded, but had merely paused on encountering the bodies of its fallen kindred and the hellish slime inscription above them. We could never know what that demon message was—but those burials at Lake's camp had shown how much importance the beings attached to their dead. Our recklessly used torch now revealed ahead of us the large open cavern where various ways converged, and we were glad to be leaving those morbid palimpsest sculptures—almost felt even when scarcely seen—behind. Another thought which the advent of the cave inspired was the possibility of losing our pursuer at this bewildering focus of large galleries. There were several of the blind albino penguins in the open space, and it seemed clear that their fear of the oncoming entity was extreme to the point of unaccountability. If at that point we dimmed our torch to the very lowest limit of traveling need, keeping it strictly in front of us, the frightened squawking motions of the huge birds in the mist might muffle our footfalls, screen our true course, and somehow set up a false lead. Amidst the churning, spiraling fog, the littered and unglistening floor of the main tunnel beyond this point, as differing from the other morbidly polished burrows, could hardly form a highly distinguishing feature; even, so far as we could conjecture, for those indicated special senses which made the Old Ones partly, though imperfectly, independent of light in emergencies. In fact, we were somewhat apprehensive lest we go astray ourselves in our haste. For we had, of course, decided to keep straight on toward the dead city; since the consequences of loss in those unknown foothill honeycombings would be unthinkable.

The fact that we survived and emerged is sufficient proof that the thing did take a wrong gallery whilst we providentially hit on the right one. The penguins alone could not have saved us, but in conjunction with the mist they seem to have done so. Only a benign fate kept the curling vapors thick enough at the right moment, for they were constantly shifting and threatening to vanish. Indeed, they did lift for a second just before we emerged from the nauseously re-sculptured tunnel into the cave; so that we actually caught one first and only half-glimpse of the oncoming entity as we cast a final, desperately fearful glance backward before dimming the torch and mixing with the penguins in the hope of dodging pursuit. If the fate which screened us was benign, that which gave us the half-glimpse was infinitely the opposite; for to that flash of semi-vision can be traced a full half of the horror which has ever since haunted us.

Our exact motive in looking back again was perhaps no more than the immemorial instinct of the pursued to gauge the nature and course of its pursuer; or perhaps it was an automatic attempt to answer a subconscious question raised by one of our senses. In the midst of our flight, with all our faculties centered on the problem of escape, we were in no condition to observe and analyze details; yet even so, our latent brain cells must have wondered at the message brought them by our nostrils. Afterward we realized what it was—that our retreat from the fetid slime-coating on those headless obstructions, and the coincident approach of the pursuing entity, had not brought us the exchange of stenches which logic called for. In the neighborhood of the prostrate things that new and lately unexplainable fetor had been wholly dominant; but by this time, it ought to have largely given place to the nameless stench associated with those others. This it had not done—for instead, the newer and less bearable smell was now virtually undiluted, and growing more and more poisonously insistent each second.

So we glanced back—simultaneously, it would appear; though no doubt the incipient motion of one prompted the imitation of the other. As we did so we flashed both torches full strength at the momentarily thinned mist; either from sheer primitive anxiety to see all we could, or in a less primitive but equally unconscious effort to dazzle the entity before we dimmed our light and dodged among the penguins of the labyrinth-center ahead. Unhappy act! Not Orpheus himself, or Lot's wife, paid much more dearly for a backward glance. And again came that shocking, wide-ranged piping—*"Tekeli-li! Tekeli-li!"*

I might as well be frank—even if I cannot bear to be quite direct—in stating what we saw; though at the time we felt that it was not to be admitted even to each other. The words reaching the reader can never even suggest the awfulness of the sight itself. It crippled our consciousness so completely that I wonder we had the residual sense to dim our torches as planned, and to strike the right tunnel toward the dead city. Instinct alone must have carried us through—perhaps better than reason could have done; though if that was what saved us, we paid a high price. Of reason we certainly had little enough left.

Danforth was totally unstrung, and the first thing I remember of the rest of the journey was hearing him lightheadedly chant an hysterical formula in which I alone of mankind could have found anything but insane irrelevance. It reverberated in falsetto echoes among the squawks of the penguins; reverberated through the vaultings ahead, and—thank God—

through the now empty vaultings behind. He could not have begun it at once—else we would not have been alive and blindly racing. I shudder to think of what a shade of difference in his nervous reactions might have brought.

"South Station Under—Washington Under—Park Street Under-Kendall—Central—Harvard. . . ." The poor fellow was chanting the familiar stations of the Boston-Cambridge tunnel that burrowed through our peaceful native soil thousands of miles away in New England, yet to me the ritual had neither irrelevance nor home-feeling. It had only horror, because I knew unerringly the monstrous, nefandous analogy that had suggested it. We had expected, upon looking back, to see a terrible and incredible moving entity if the mists were thin enough; but of that entity we had formed a clear idea. What we did see—for the mists were indeed all too malignly thinned—was something altogether different, and immeasurably more hideous and detestable. It was the utter, objective embodiment of the fantastic novelist's "thing that should not be"; and its nearest comprehensible analogue is a vast, onrushing subway train as one sees it from a station platform—the great black front looming colossally out of infinite subterranean distance, constellated with strangely colored lights and filling the prodigious burrow as a piston fills a cylinder.

But we were not on a station platform. We were on the track ahead as the nightmare, plastic column of fetid black iridescence oozed tightly onward through its fifteen-foot sinus, gathering unholy speed and driving before it a spiral, re-thickening cloud of the pallid abyss-vapor. It was a terrible, indescribable thing vaster than any subway train—a shapeless congeries of protoplasmic bubbles, faintly self-luminous, and with myriads of temporary eyes forming and un-forming as pustules of greenish light all over the tunnel-filling front that bore down upon us, crushing the frantic penguins and slithering over the glistening floor that it and its kind had swept so evilly free of all litter. Still came that eldritch, mocking cry—*"Tekeli-li! Tekeli-li!"* and at last we remembered that the demoniac Shoggoths—given life, thought, and plastic organ patterns solely by the Old Ones, and having no language save that which the dot-groups expressed—had likewise no voice save the imitated accents of their bygone masters.

Chapter 12

Danforth and I have recollections of emerging into the great sculptured hemisphere and of threading our back trail through the Cyclopean rooms and corridors of the dead city; yet these are purely dream fragments involving no memory of volition, details, or physical exertion. It was as if we floated in a nebulous world or dimension without time, causation, or orientation. The gray half-daylight of the vast circular space sobered us somewhat; but we did not go near those cached sledges or look again at poor Gedney and the dog. They have a strange and titanic mausoleum, and I hope the end of this planet will find them still undisturbed.

It was while struggling up the colossal spiral incline that we first felt the terrible fatigue and short breath which our race through the thin plateau air had produced; but not even fear of collapse could make us pause before reaching the normal outer realm of sun and sky. There was something vaguely appropriate about our departure from those buried epochs; for as we wound our panting way up the sixty-foot cylinder of primal masonry, we glimpsed beside us a continuous procession of heroic sculptures in the dead race's early and undecayed technique—a farewell from the Old Ones, written fifty million years ago.

Finally scrambling out at the top, we found ourselves on a great mound of tumbled blocks, with the curved walls of higher stonework rising westward, and the brooding peaks of the great mountains showing beyond the more crumbled structures toward the east. The low Antarctic sun of midnight peered redly from the southern horizon through rifts in the jagged ruins, and the terrible age and deadness of the nightmare city seemed all the starker by contrast with such relatively known and accustomed things as the features of the polar landscape. The sky above was a churning and opalescent mass of tenuous ice-vapors, and the cold clutched at our vitals. Wearily resting the outfit-bags to which we had instinctively clung throughout our desperate flight, we rebuttoned our heavy garments for the stumbling climb down the mound and the walk through the aeon-old stone maze to the foothills where our aeroplane waited. Of what had set us fleeing from that darkness of earth's secret and archaic gulfs we said nothing at all.

In less than a quarter of an hour we had found the steep grade to the foothills—the probable ancient terrace—by which we had descended, and could see the dark bulk of our great plane amidst the sparse ruins on the rising slope ahead. Halfway uphill toward our goal we paused for a momentary breathing spell, and turned to look again at the fantastic tangle of incredible stone shapes below us—once more outlined mystically against an unknown west. As we did so we saw that the sky beyond had lost its morning haziness; the restless ice-vapors having moved up to the zenith, where their mocking outlines seemed on the point of settling into some bizarre pattern which they feared to make quite definite or conclusive.

There now lay revealed on the ultimate white horizon behind the grotesque city a dim, elfin line of pinnacled violet whose needle-pointed heights loomed dreamlike against the beckoning rose-color of the western sky. Up toward this shimmering rim sloped the ancient table-land, the depressed course of the bygone river traversing it as an irregular ribbon of shadow. For a second, we gasped in admiration of the scene's unearthly cosmic beauty, and then vague horror began to creep into our souls. For this far violet line could be nothing else than the terrible mountains of the forbidden land—highest of earth's peaks and focus of earth's evil; harborers of nameless horrors and Archaean secrets; shunned and prayed to by those who feared to carve their meaning; untrodden by any living thing on earth, but visited by the sinister lightnings and sending strange beams across the plains in the polar night—beyond doubt the unknown archetype of that dreaded Kadath in the Cold Waste beyond abhorrent Leng, whereof primal legends hint evasively. We were the first human beings ever to see them—and I hope to God we may be the last.

If the sculptured maps and pictures in that pre-human city had told truly, these cryptic violet mountains could not be much less than three hundred miles away; yet none the less sharply did their dim elfin essence appear above that remote and snowy rim, like the serrated edge of a monstrous alien planet about to rise into unaccustomed heavens. Their height, then, must have been tremendous beyond all comparison—carrying them up into tenuous atmospheric strata peopled only by such gaseous wraiths as rash flyers have barely lived to whisper of after unexplainable falls. Looking at them, I thought nervously of certain sculptured hints of what the great bygone river had washed down into the city from their accursed slopes—and wondered how much sense and how much folly had lain in the fears of those Old Ones who carved them so reticently. I recalled how their northerly end must come near the coast at Queen Mary Land, where even at that moment Sir Douglas Mawson's expedition was doubtless working less than a thousand miles away; and hoped that no evil fate would give Sir Douglas and his men a glimpse of what might lie beyond the protecting coastal range. Such thoughts formed a measure of my overwrought condition at the time—and Danforth seemed to be even worse.

Yet long before we had passed the great star-shaped ruin and reached our plane, our fears had become transferred to the lesser but vast-enough range whose recrossing lay ahead of us. From these foothills the black, ruin-crusted slopes reared up starkly and hideously against the east, again reminding us of those strange Asian paintings of Nicholas Roerich; and when we thought of the frightful amorphous entities that might have pushed their fetidly squirming way even to the topmost hollow pinnacles, we could not face without panic the prospect of again sailing by those suggestive skyward cave-mouths where the wind made sounds like an evil musical piping over a wide range. To make matters worse, we saw distinct traces of local mist around several of the summits—as poor Lake must have done when he made that early mistake about volcanism—and thought shiveringly of that kindred mist from which we had just escaped; of that, and of the blasphemous, horror-fostering abyss whence all such vapors came.

All was well with the plane, and we clumsily hauled on our heavy flying furs. Danforth got the engine started without trouble, and we made a very smooth take-off over the nightmare city. Below us the primal Cyclopean masonry spread out as it had done when first we saw it—so short, yet infinitely long, a time ago—and we began rising and turning to test the wind for our crossing through the pass. At a very high level there must have been great disturbance, since the ice-dust clouds of the zenith were doing all sorts of fantastic things; but at twenty-four thousand feet, the height we needed for the pass, we found navigation quite practicable. As we drew close to the jutting peaks the wind's strange piping again became manifest, and I could see Danforth's hands trembling at the controls. Rank amateur that I was, I thought at that moment that I might be a better navigator than he in effecting the dangerous crossing between pinnacles; and when I made motions to change seats and take over his duties he did not protest. I tried to keep all my skill and self-possession about me, and stared at the sector of reddish farther sky betwixt the walls of the pass—resolutely refusing to pay attention to the puffs of mountain-top vapor, and wishing that I had wax-stopped ears like Ulysses' men off the Siren's coast to keep that disturbing windpiping from my consciousness.

But Danforth, released from his piloting and keyed up to a dangerous nervous pitch, could not keep quiet. I felt him turning and wriggling about as he looked back at the terrible receding city, ahead at the cave-riddled, cube-barnacled peaks, sidewise at the bleak sea of snowy, rampart-strewn foothills, and upward at the seething, grotesquely clouded sky. It was then, just as I was trying to steer safely through the pass, that his mad shrieking brought us so close to disaster by shattering my tight hold on myself and causing me to fumble helplessly with the controls for a moment. A second afterward my resolution triumphed and we made the crossing safely—yet I am afraid that Danforth will never be the same again.

I have said that Danforth refused to tell me what final horror made him scream out so insanely—a horror which, I feel sadly sure, is mainly responsible for his present breakdown. We had snatches of shouted conversation above the wind's piping and the engine's buzzing as we reached the safe side of the range and swooped slowly down toward the camp, but that had mostly to do with the pledges of secrecy we had made as we prepared to leave the nightmare city. Certain things, we had agreed, were not for people to know and discuss lightly—and I would not speak of them now but for the need of heading off that Starkweather-Moore Expedition, and others, at any cost. It is absolutely necessary, for the peace and safety of mankind, that some of earth's dark, dead corners and unplumbed depths be let alone; lest sleeping abnormalities wake to resurgent life, and blasphemously surviving nightmares squirm and splash out of their black lairs to newer and wider conquests.

All that Danforth has ever hinted is that the final horror was a mirage. It was not, he declares, anything connected with the cubes and caves of those echoing, vaporous, wormily-honeycombed mountains of madness which we crossed; but a single fantastic, demoniac glimpse, among the churning zenith-clouds, of what lay back of those other violet westward mountains which the Old Ones had shunned and feared. It is very probable that the thing was a sheer delusion born of the previous stresses we had passed through, and of the actual though unrecognized mirage of the dead transmontane city experienced near Lake's camp the day before; but it was so real to Danforth that he suffers from it still.

He has on rare occasions whispered disjointed and irresponsible things about "The black pit," "the carven rim," "the proto-Shoggoths," "the windowless solids with five dimensions," "the nameless cylinder," "the elder Pharos," "Yog-Sothoth," "the primal white jelly," "the color out of space," "the wings," "the eyes in darkness," "the moon-ladder," "the original, the eternal, the undying," and other bizarre conceptions; but when he is fully himself, he repudiates all this and attributes it to his curious and macabre reading of earlier years. Danforth, indeed, is known to be among the few who have ever dared go completely through that worm-riddled copy of the *Necronomicon* kept under lock and key in the college library.

The higher sky, as we crossed the range, was surely vaporous and disturbed enough; and although I did not see the zenith, I can well imagine that its swirls of ice dust may have taken strange forms. Imagination, knowing how vividly distant scenes can sometimes be reflected, refracted, and magnified by such layers of restless cloud, might easily have supplied the rest—and, of course, Danforth did not hint any of these specific horrors till after his memory had had a chance to draw on his bygone reading. He could never have seen so much in one instantaneous glance.

At the time, his shrieks were confined to the repetition of a single, mad word of all too obvious source: *"Tekeli-li! Tekeli-li!"*

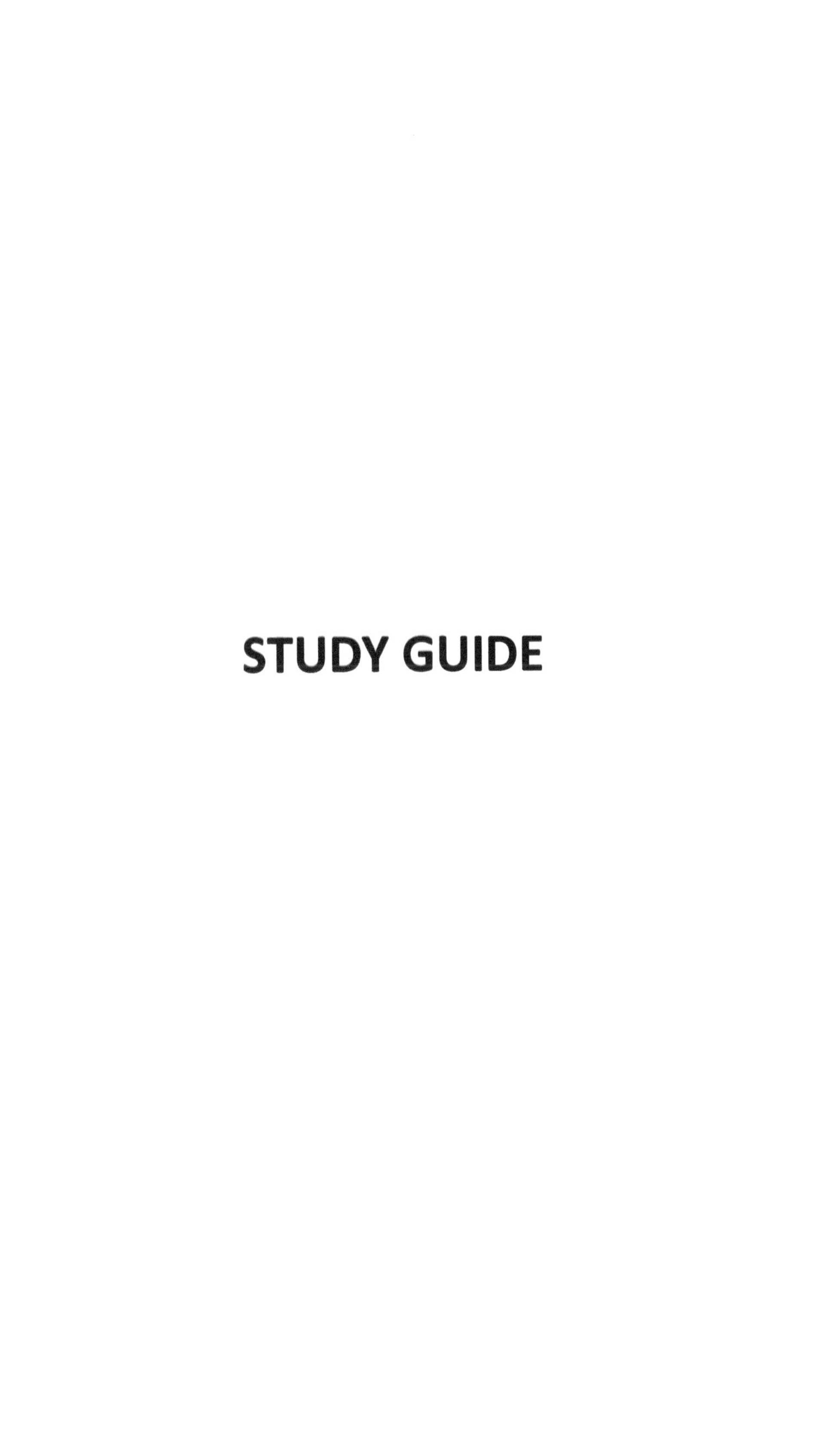

STUDY GUIDE

The Characters of the Story

Prof. William Dyer: A professor of geology at Miskatonic University, in the mythical town of Arkham, Massachusetts, and a leader of the ill-fated Pabodie Expedition to Antarctica in September 1930. He is the narrator of this novella. Only his last name is mentioned in the story, but he resurfaces—and his first name is revealed—in Lovecraft's *The Shadow Out of Time.* In that tale, Dyer accompanies an expedition to the Great Sandy Desert in Australia in search of another ancient civilization. He is portrayed as the consummate scientist who manages to stay calm and collected in the face of astounding discoveries and unspeakable horrors encountered by the expedition.

Danforth: A graduate student at Miskatonic University who joins the Pabodie Expedition to Antarctica. His first name is not mentioned in the story. He accompanies Dyer on a survey flight to the Plateau of Leng, where they find evidence of an alien civilization that thrived in the icy region eons ago. While searching the ruins of an abandoned city, the two men encounter innumerable horrors, and as they flee for their lives and depart the desolate mountain range, Danforth sees something that drives him to a permanent state of madness. Lovecraft introduces this character as "a great reader of bizarre material," and makes allusions to Edgar Allan Poe and the fabled *Necronomicon.* The story ends with Danforth lapsing into fits of madness and incoherent babbling. However, according to a short story published three decades later by American writer Fritz Leiber, he recovered after undergoing treatment with experimental drugs, but he never spoke of the horror he saw in the mountains of Antarctica that drove him mad. In Leiber's story, Danforth recovers and becomes a psychology professor at Miskatonic University.

Frank Pabodie: A faculty member of Miskatonic University's engineering department, Prof. Pabodie invented a drill for the expedition to Antarctica that was described as revolutionary—it was "unique and radical in its lightness, portability, and capacity...capable of drilling through strata of varying hardness." In addition, Pabodie developed "fuel-warming and quick-starting devices" to the expedition's four aircraft. Fans and students of Lovecraft's substantial body of writings suggest that the name "Pabodie" is an alternate spelling of Peabody, perhaps named after the Peabody Museum in Salem, with which Lovecraft was familiar.

Lake: A biology professor at Miskatonic University. He joins the Pabodie Expedition and is credited with discovering the Mountains of Madness as a result of his insistence on undertaking a northwestward prospecting trip, where he discovers enigmatic fossils from an ancient, extraterrestrial race that he calls the "Elder Ones" of "Old Ones," based on their resemblance to "certain monsters of primal myth" described in the *Necronomicon*. Lake excitedly reports the details of his astounding discovery to the base camp, claiming that what he has found is proof that alien civilizations have come and gone from planet earth over millions of years and elatedly declaring that what he has discovered will "mean to biology what Einstein has meant to mathematics and physics." The excitement over his fabulous discovery turns to horror, however, when eight of the Old Ones prove to be very much alive rather than fossils and slaughter Lake, his companions, and his sledge dogs.

Atwood: A physics professor at Miskatonic University, as well as an astute meteorologist. He accompanies Lake on his prospecting excursion and is slaughtered by the Old Ones.

Chapter 1 Review

This science-fiction/horror novella begins with the narrator, who is later revealed to be Professor Dyer, advising readers that the information he is about to reveal is of the utmost importance and great urgency. He cautions that these revelations are so extraordinary many will question the authenticity of his report. He opines that it is unfortunate obscure researchers such as himself and his associates may be dismissed because they are affiliated with a small university.

Dyer recalls that a remarkable drilling apparatus had been designed by his colleague at Miskatonic University, Prof. Frank H. Pabodie. The drill was an amazing feat of technology for the present day, and the members of his expedition were excited about the groundbreaking research the new tool would enable them to undertake in their search for fossils at a remote mountain range in the Antarctic. Dyer recalls that he had hoped their findings would yield new knowledge of the evolution of the land and environment in the vast, unexplored region. He goes on to explain that a second expedition—the Starkweather-Moore party—is planning to explore the area, and he feels compelled to dissuade them from this mission so they will not encounter the horrors that befell his own ill-fated expedition.

Dyer reflects back on his trek—the Pabodie Expedition—stating that it was well-equipped and well-funded. They set out on the journey by sea, and as they sailed closer to the icy desolation of the Antarctic, the plunging temperatures proved challenging for the crew. Dyer saw his first mirage during this time, visualizing icebergs around their ships that became the battlements of vast cosmic castles. After nearly two months at sea, the expedition finally sees land as they near the Admiralty mountain range discovered by Ross.

Dyer has a sense of foreboding as the ships approach their destination. After slow progress and more weeks at sea, they finally dock, and the crew sets foot on land in McMurdo Sound. Dyer recalls that the sights in this surreal ice world reminded him of an Antarctic scene described in Edgar Allen Poe's only long story, *Arthur Gordon Pym.*

The expedition sets up camp near the slopes of a towering mountain range and goes to work. The researchers chisel, dynamite, and drill into the icy plateau in search of clues to the region's primordial history. They find a rich assortment of fossils confirming the existence of plant and sea life that thrived in the region eons ago, as well as some pieces of slate with inexplicable, irregular triangle patterns that they agree warrant require further investigation.

Discussion Prompts

1. Describe how Lovecraft builds suspense in the opening chapter of the story by relying on the narrator's account. Explain why this storytelling technique is effective, or if you don't think it is, elaborate.

2. What kind of device did Prof. Pabodie design, and how did it help the expedition in its groundbreaking research?

Chapter Quiz

1.01. The narrator of this story is Professor __________.
a) Dwyer
b) Dyer
c) Corbin
d) Pabodie

1.02. Which university is the narrator of the story affiliated with?
a) Harvard
b) Chesapeake University
c) Miskatonic University
d) Monster University
e) None of these answers are correct.

1.03. What is the narrator's profession?
a) geologist
b) archaeologist
c) math teacher
d) journalist

1.04. The Miskatonic expedition's destination is __________.
a) mountains in the Antarctic
b) a mountain range in Canada
c) the deep waters of the Atlantic
d) the mountains of a faraway island

1.05. Who developed the new drilling equipment that the expedition hopes will help them make discoveries about the region's distant past?
a) Prof. Smithson
b) Prof. Dyer
c) Prof. Pabodie
d) The author does not reveal who developed it.

1.06. What features made Pabodie's new drilling apparatus noteworthy?

a) its light weight
b) its portability
c) its ability to drill through strata of varying hardness
d) All of these answers are correct.

1.07. How many airplanes were needed to transport the expedition?

a) seven
b) one
c) four
d) five

1.08. How many sledges were needed to pull the drilling apparatus over the icy tundra?

a) seven
b) three
c) four
d) five
e) ten

1.09. What did the Pabodie Expedition hope to find during its trip to the frozen continent of Antarctica?

a) animals that could survive the harsh winters
b) supplies to help them on their journey
c) materials that would explain more about the earth's past
d) All of these answers are correct.

1.10. How many assistants participated in the Miskatonic expedition?

a) four
b) twenty-six
c) sixteen
d) eleven
e) fifteen

1.11. How was the Pabodie Expedition financed?

a) Nathaniel Derby Pickman Foundation
b) a private law firm
c) Professor Dyer's mother
d) The British government
e) a grant from Miskatonic University

1.12. What date did the expedition embark on its journey?
a) the last week of September
b) the day after Thanksgiving
c) Professor Pabodie's birthday
d) September 2, 1930

1.13. Had anyone on the Pabodie Expedition visited the Antarctic before?
a) only the ship captains
b) two of the professors
c) one of the assistants
d) This was the first trip for everyone.

1.14. What was the date that the expedition caught a glimpse of land as they approached their destination?
a) the day before Halloween
b) July 12
c) July 21
d) October 26

1.15. When was the expedition finally able to set foot on land?
a) just after dark
b) November 8
c) October 26

1.16. What great poet does Danforth evoke when he sees lava on a snowy slope?
a) Edgar Allen Poe
b) John Keats
c) Walt Whitman
d) Cummings

1.17. When did the expedition arrive at Ross Island?
a) shortly after midnight
b) shortly before midnight
c) after dinner
d) noon

1.18. The expedition's base ship was named __________.
a) The Majestic
b) The Arkham
c) The Antarctica

1.19. What is the name of the second ship in the Pabodie Expedition?

a) The Waterdipper
b) The Gin and Tonic
c) The Miskatonic
d) The Antarctic

1.20. How many dogs accompanied the expedition on their journey?

a) 55 Alaskan sledge dogs
b) 14 German Shepherds and 42 Mastiff
c) 50 French Poodles
d) 50 dogs of mixed breeds

1.21. How tall is Mount Nansen?

a) 5,000 feet
b) 10,000 feet
c) 15,000 feet
d) 20,000 feet

1.22. Who ascended Mt. Nansen with Prof. Pabodie on Dec. 13-15?

a) Gedney and Carroll
b) Pabodie and Gedney
c) Carroll and Dyer
d) Pabodie went alone

1.23. What did the expedition members drink to offset the steady diet of tinned and salted food?

a) lime juice
b) Pepto Bismol
c) carrot juice
d) vodka

1.24. When the expedition discovered oddly marked fragments, how old did they estimate these artifacts to be?

a) 100,000 years
b) 500,000 to 550,000 years
c) 500 million years
d) less than 1 million years

Chapter 2 Review

The expedition moves further into the northwestern regions, exploring a vast frozen territory that no human has ever seen before. As they uncover more and more of the Archaean slate with strange markings, Lake decides to take a prospecting expedition further out to bore and drill for a week. He asks Dyer to accompany him, but Dyer declines and remains at the base camp with Pabodie and five other men.

Lake identifies a new site and begins drilling. He makes discoveries that he can't wait to share with the others upon his return, so he sends back a series of messages that convey his growing excitement. Despite warnings about the possibility of dangerous high winds, Lake loads his discoveries on the plane and commences the return flight to the base to rejoin Pabodie and Dyer. During his flight, Lake relays the discovery of a mountain range with two smoking cones that is higher than any they have ever seen before. That interesting news makes Dyer wish he had agreed to accompany Lake after all.

As the powerful winds intensified, one of the planes accompanying Lake was forced down. After an emergency landing, Lake's team transferred the equipment to the other planes and commenced repairs on the damaged plane. Lake decided to scout the area and continued to send back relays detailing his discoveries. He described what he saw in the terrain and those at the base camp stayed awake to listen. Dyer agreed to join Lake as soon as he could work out a gas plan to bring out additional supplies. The plan was to establish a new camp at the base of the curious new mountain range Lake had discovered.

Lake and his team began setting up a camp where the plane had gone down. He continues to relay descriptions of the treacherously windswept terrain. The next morning, the men agree that Lake will send one of his planes to come for Dyer, Pabodie, and the five others.

Lake begins blasting and drilling at a site near his camp, and before long, his crew is startled to uncover a cave. Lake sends a series of excited relays to the base camp detailing the group's findings, and he predicts that what he has discovered "will mean to biology what Einstein has meant to mathematics and physics". Lake observes that the fossils he digs up appear to have wounds that he cannot attribute to any known animal from any period. He decides to search deeper in the cave. As he hacks away at the stalactites, he reports that the dogs are becoming agitated, and he ascribes this to the possibility that the dogs were picking up a peculiar odor from the rock.

After digging still deeper, around 10:15 p.m., Lake reports that his team has excavated a monstrous, barrel-shaped fossil that is very well preserved.

He says that the creature reminds him of the terrible things from the fabled Elder Things in the *Necronomicon,* and he notes that the dogs are getting harder to handle the deeper into the cave they go. They are extremely agitated and bark incessantly.

At 11:30, Lake sends an enthusiastic report that connects the odd barrel creature to the patterns they have been finding in the rocks. More than a dozen of the creatures were unearthed, and Lake gave a very detailed description of them. They carefully loaded the fossils to transport back to camp. Once there, it became necessary to set up a separate area for the dogs because they were so agitated.

Lake began dissecting one of the creatures immediately and found that the internal organs were wholly intact. He had difficulty determining whether the fossilized life forms had been vegetable or animal, as they appeared to have characteristics of both. He concluded that they must have had more than five senses.

When he had completed his research for the night, he decided to get some much-needed sleep. The dogs were still restive and barking incessantly, so Lake covered the remaining specimens with a tarp hoping that it would ameliorate the scent and calm the animals. After thanking Pabodie once again for creating a fantastic drilling apparatus which made these discoveries possible, he signed off for the night.

Discussion Prompts

1. What discovery did Lake and his team report that made Prof. Dyer regret that he had not come along on the excursion?

2. What is Lovecraft hinting at, or what point do you think he is trying to make, when he repeatedly credits the drilling apparatus for making Lake's discoveries possible?

Chapter Quiz

2.01. When did Lake's party do their preliminary sledging and boring?

a) January 11
b) February 2
c) January 1
d) January 11-18

2.02. How many dogs were lost during Lake's excursion?

a) two
b) all of them
c) none of them
d) twenty-two

2.03. How many men accompanied Lake on his excursion?

a) seven
b) seventeen
c) three
d) nine

2.04. What did the narrator of the story say it was unwise to be without?

a) friends
b) alcohol
c) transportation
d) books

2.05. On what date did Lake make his most exciting discovery?

a) January 12
b) January 1
c) January 2
d) January 22

2.06. What time was the first wireless message from Lake received?

a) 6:00 a.m.
b) around noon
c) 6:00 p.m.
d) well after dark

2.07. How far away was Lake's drilling site from Dyer's base camp?

a) 300 miles
b) 350 miles
c) 500 miles
d) 30 miles

2.08. During Lake's flight, what observation did he make at 10:05 p.m.?

a) a building made of clay
b) an alien lifeform
c) a large mountain range
d) a piece of candy

2.09. What bad news did Lake relay from his camp around 10:05 p.m.?

a) Moulton's plane crashed into a mountain.
b) Moulton's plane was forced down on a plateau.
c) Moulton had a stroke and was unable to pilot the plane.
d) Moulton refused to land the plane.

2.10. Where did Lake decide to camp while the downed plane was being repaired?

a) at the location where it went down
b) in a tree near the river
c) in a nearby ravine
d) as far away as he could get

2.11. What environmental factors worried Lake during his flight?

a) the freezing rain
b) the heavy winds
c) the extreme darkness
d) all of the above

2.12. What covered the roof and floor of the cave that Lake discovered?

a) stalactites and stalagmites
b) a pungent, green cave mold
c) glowing spheres
d) a dead flock of black penguins
e) None of these answers are correct.

2.13. What geological age did Lake conclude the newest fossils in the cave were from?

a) the Stone Age
b) the Golden Age
c) the Palionethic Age
d) the Oligocene Age
e) the Neolithic era

2.14. During Lake's journey, he sent out a series of communications. What was the substance of these messages?

a) details about the fossils they were finding
b) unintelligible babbling
c) questions about the map
d) urgent pleas for food and more fuel

2.15. To whom did Lake want to convey the importance of his scientific findings?

a) the British Archaeological Society
b) the press
c) the head of the geology department at his university
d) the next expedition

2.16. How many barrel specimens did Lake's expedition unearth?
a) four
b) fourteen
c) forty
d) forty-four

2.17. When did Lake plan to dissect one of the creatures he had excavated?
a) He didn't want to dissect them.
b) first thing in the morning
c) as soon as they got back to camp
d) immediately when Dyer arrived

2.18. What color was the thick fluid that oozed from the creature?
a) green
b) greenish-blue
c) blue
d) purple

2.19. How many lobes did Lake observe in the creature's brain?
a) four
b) five
c) six
d) seven

Chapter 3 Review

No one slept well that night between the excitement of the discovery and the fierce winds. The next morning, McTighe was unable to communicate with Lake's camp, which he attributed to some electrical disturbance in the air. By evening, with still no word from Lake, the researchers' concern intensified. Dyer decided to take the fifth plane from the supply cache and set out to search for Lake's team.

As the rescue mission got underway, Dyer felt a sinking sense of despair, made worse by the fierce winds and surreal landscape below. His description of the terrain is bleak. He regrets that he ever read books such as the *Necronomicon* or talked so much about folklore with colleagues at the university. His recollections of those books and conversations merely heightened the sense of dread he felt as he gazed out at the desolate terrain and added to the menacing symbolism that he attributed to it.

When the search party located Lake's outpost, they found that the wind had inflicted heavy damage on the camp. There were no signs of life in the area, and the nearby corral that had been built to contain the dogs had been ripped apart inexplicably. The men closed off the cave that Lake's team had discovered and decided to leave that place as soon as possible. Dyer composed a calm and careful relay back to the *Arkham* about what they had found at the deserted outpost.

Danforth and Dyer undertook a scouting mission the next day, and they subsequently agreed to keep their drawings, photos, and much of the information they uncovered on this unsettling trek between themselves. Upon their return, they repaired what they could and packed up what little remained to salvage from Lake's outpost, and then headed back to the base camp. There, they gathered the remainder of their equipment and supplies to take back to the ships and begin the long journey home.

Upon their return to the States, Dyer and his fellow researchers kept most of their findings under wraps, and tried to discourage any further exploration of the Antarctic. Danforth went mad, but despite suffering a nervous breakdown, he remained faithful and did not reveal any of the dark secrets from that trip to his doctors. Dyer does not expect that he will be successful at preventing future expeditions to that terrible place in the Antarctic, observing that "human curiosity is undying." When he learns of the upcoming Starkweather-Moore expedition to the Antarctic, he is alarmed and fears that if they succeed at digging deep enough within the mountains of madness, they may unearth something so horrific that it will bring an end to the world as we know it.

Discussion Prompts:

1. Why do Dyer and Danforth decide to keep their findings to themselves after scouting the area around Lake's outpost?

2. Dyer observes that "human curiosity is undying." Explain what this means and give three examples of human curiosity persisting despite the threat of great danger or disaster.

Chapter Quiz:

3.01. How many planes escorted Lake on his doomed sub-expedition?

a) four
b) five
c) one
d) six

3.02. How many hours of sleep did the men at the base camp get before they went out to search for Lake?

a) none
b) two
c) three
d) four

3.03. On what date did Dyer's party go out searching for Lake's group?

a) December 2
b) January 25
c) January 29
d) February 4

3.04. How many dogs did the search party bring to Lake's camp?

a) two
b) four
c) seven
d) twenty

3.05. What was the weather on the morning that the search party set out for Lake's camp?

a) clear
b) mild in temperature
c) fairly quiet
d) All of these answers are correct.

3.06. How long did it take the rescuers to reach Lake's camp?

a) four hours
b) four and a half hours
c) fourteen hours
d) it took all night

3.07. Why was the rescue flight in this chapter burned into Dyer's memory?

a) He hated flying.
b) It was the last time he drank coffee.
c) It marked the loss of his sense of peace and balance.
d) He felt an overwhelming sense of guilt.

3.08. What name did Dyer give to the dark spires that he saw?

a) chaotic ravens of death
b) dark spires of evil
c) mountains of madness
d) mountains and molehills

3.09. How did Dyer describe what the mountain slopes overlooked?

a) some accursed ultimate abyss
b) a beautiful frozen lake
c) the whole world
d) the deepest snow he had ever seen

3.10. Why did Dyer recount this story despite his vow to keep it secret?

a) He wanted his name to be remembered in history.
b) He wanted to warn others.
c) He had a nervous breakdown and confessed to his doctor.
d) The university paid him to write a documentary.

3.11. How many of the dogs that accompanied Lake's party survived?

a) only the dachshund
b) two
c) none
d) Dyer's favorite husky and one other

3.12. How many intact specimens remained at Lake's outpost when Dyer and the other searchers arrived?

a) none
b) two
c) four

3.13. Why was Dyer so careful about the wording in his relays to the *Arkham*?

a) He did not want to alarm the public.
b) He knew the ship's crew did not speak English well.
c) He was making the story up and trying not to contradict himself.
d) He was in a state of shock and having difficulty remembering.

3.14. What did Danforth think he saw on the scouting tour with Dyer?

a) He saw his own reflection.
b) He has never told anyone what he saw.
c) He saw two of the missing dogs.
d) He saw a portal into the past.

3.15. What were the two ships that would take the expedition back to the United States?

a) the Flotsam and Jetsam
b) the Old Man and the Sea
c) the Arch and the Miskatonic
d) the Arkham and the Miskatonic

3.16. Which character from the story had a nervous breakdown upon returning to the U.S.?

a) Wentworth
b) Danforth
c) Dyer
d) Pabodie

3.17. What is the name of the expedition party that intends to undertake a follow-up trip to Antarctica?

a) Arkham-Wentworth expedition
b) Fisher-Price expedition
c) Starkweather-Moore expedition
d) Merriweather-Moore expedition

Chapter 4 Review

Dyer's mind drifts back to the expedition and the gruesome scene they had encountered at Lake's camp. He acknowledges that he left out many of the details hoping to "let hints stand for actual facts." He mentions that when his search party found the sledge dogs' remains, they noticed that one dog was missing. He continues to discuss the state of the camp and ponders the details that he left out about the condition of the dead men and dogs. All of the bodies were inexplicably and viciously torn and mangled, Dyer says, and it appeared that they had all died from strangulation or laceration.

Dyer theorized that the dogs had started the trouble, based on the condition of their corral. It seemed to have been torn apart from the inside out. He believed that the winds had driven the dogs mad, and the odor from the frozen creatures that the expedition had unearthed sent them into a frenzy. He reflected further on the scene uncovered at the camp and confessed that large chunks of solid tissue had been cut away from the bodies, as if a butcher had removed them. He also had noted traces of salt on the ground near the horrific scene.

Upon entering Lake's dissecting tent, Dyer observed that there was no creature on the table under a tarp as Lake had left it. Instead, strewn about on and around the table were fleshy chunks dissected from a man and a dog. There were some strange smudges, and several items were missing, as was the bodies of Gedney and one of the dogs.

Dyer's group took photographs of the gruesome carnage at the camp. They conducted a thorough search but failed to find any trace of Gedney, the missing dog, or any of the other items that had vanished inexplicably from the site. Danforth and Dyer had conducted an aerial survey of the surrounding terrain, making an ascent to the top of the mountain. Once there, they gazed out across a terrifying alien earth which presumably had never been seen by human eyes.

Discussion Prompts:

1. How does Lovecraft's use of situational irony in this chapter enhance the suspense of the story?

2. Why did Dyer and Danforth continue their survey despite the horror they found at Lake's dissection tent?

Chapter Quiz:

4.01. Professor Dyer was an expert when it came to flying a plane.

a) True
b) False

4.02. When they counted the remains of the dead dogs, how many were missing?

a) one
b) two
c) three
d) four

4.03. Whose body was missing when Dyer and Danforth performed the search?

a) Pabodie
b) Gedney
c) Danforth
d) Wentworth

4.04. Where were most of the bodies found during the search of Lake's camp?

a) in an igloo house
b) in a corral built for the dogs
c) under the tarp in Lake's dissecting room
d) in one of the airplane shelters

4.05. What item or items were missing from Lake's dissecting tent?

a) a gas stove
b) fur suits
c) Lake's anatomical instruments
d) All of these answers are correct.

4.06. What evidence of the gruesome scene at Lake's camp was Dyer able to take back with him?

a) footprints
b) blood spatter
c) photographs
d) audio tapes

4.07. What did Dyer plan to do with the horrific evidence gathered at Lake's devastated outpost?

a) burn it
b) show it to the Starkweather-Moore party in the hope that it would dissuade them from returning to the Antarctic
c) send the evidence to the media
d) display the artifacts as trophies in his office

4.08. How high up did the plane take Dyer and Danforth during their aerial search of the area around Lake's outpost?

a) 23,570 feet
b) 23,500 feet
c) 35,730 feet
d) 57,320 feet

4.09. Dyer saw a half-impression of faint snow-prints in one shielded corner of the ruined enclosure during his search.

a) True
b) False

4.10. Around the mangled bodies, Dyer found an odd sprinkling of ______, which had been taken from a pillaged provision-chest on the planes.

a) boric powder
b) gun powder
c) salt
d) pepper

4.11. The covered remains of the primal monstrosity Lake had uncovered had been removed from the makeshift table in the dissecting tent.

a) True
b) False

4.12. Pabodie was driven to a nervous collapse by the horrors he had witnessed during the expedition to the Antarctic.

a) True
b) False

4.13. After the bodies of Lake's team and the dogs were examined, what did Dyer conclude was the cause of death?

a) hypothermia
b) strangulation or laceration
c) hyperthermia
d) blunt force injury

4.14. The ancient and wind-weathered rock layers that Dyer's expedition had excavated verified all of Lake's astounding bulletins.

a) True
b) False

4.15. Lake's original suspicion of smoking cones did prove to be natural, volcanic structures.

a) True

b) False

Danforth and Dyer reach the peak of the mountain and look beyond, seeing a spectacular panorama of strange cubes, towers, and ramparts that seemed to form the structure of some unknown ancient city. The incredible sight reminded Dyer of various myths he had previously read and heard about abominable snowmen, the demonic plateau of Leng, the Cthulhu cult, and the hyperborean legends. He describes the terrain in great detail and draws some speculative conclusions about how this alien civilization must have looked millions of years ago.

The two men were fascinated yet terrified by the surreal glimpse of the ancient past and wondered who might have built the city. It was unlike anything they had ever seen. They decided to try landing the plane and venture out on foot to further their discoveries. Once on the ground, they gathered surveying equipment and began to explore the nameless city. They ventured forth carefully, with heightened senses, and Dyer noticed that Danforth seemed very jumpy. The men chipped away at the rock and took samples from various structures, hoping it would help them reconstruct a full picture of the alien city lost in time.

They found a suitable entrance and decided to explore one of the larger structures. Based on their observations, Dyer surmised that whatever had brought ruin to the civilization that lived eons ago may have been foreseen and prepared for. It did not seem that the area had been deserted in a hurry. He decided it would be impossible to speculate on what might have happened here, as there were so many possibilities.

Discussion Prompts:

1. What leads Dyer to the conclusion that the ancient city had been deliberately evacuated in a bygone era?

Chapter Quiz:

5.01. How high was the table of land that the expedition found?

a) 20,000 feet
b) 25,000 feet
c) 27,000 feet
d) 37,000 feet

5.02. Before Dyer and Danforth left the rampart, they drew a dozen sketches of the area to document its remarkable, mortarless masonry.

a) True
b) False

5.03. Based on the description in this chapter, how tall were the massive stone walls of the labyrinth?

a) 10-150 feet

b) 200 feet

c) 250 feet

d) over 300 feet

5.04. What connected many of the towers to one another in the alien city?

a) a railway system

b) massive windows

c) stone arches

d) stone bridges

5.05. What did the expedition conclude had once existed in the bare area that they observed?

a) a lake

b) a creek

c) a river

d) a flowerbed

5.06. What evidence did the men take back with them from the plane trip recounted in this chapter?

a) ice picks

b) photographs

c) a sledgehammer

d) fingerprints

5.07. What did the sight of the vast alien city cause Danforth and Dyer to wonder?

a) what sort of beings had built it and who lived there

b) what happened to the slaves that had been captured

c) how was the lofty mountain formed

d) what the creatures might have done for entertainment

5.08. What did the men plan to use to help them find their way back out of the cavernous structures that they wanted to enter?

a) breadcrumbs

b) candles

c) shredded paper

d) an ice pick

5.09. What shape were many of the topographical points of interest that the expedition found?

a) crescent-shaped
b) circular
c) star-shaped
d) diamond-shaped

5.10. Who did Dyer and Danforth wish was there to help them?

a) Danforth
b) Pabodie
c) Falstead
d) Gedney

5.11. What covered many of the window structures they found in the city?

a) curtains
b) tarps
c) paper
d) shutters

5.12. The alien city was badly weather-beaten, and the glacial surface from which the towers projected was strewn with fallen blocks and debris.

a) True
b) False

5.13. The rampart was shaped like a star and approximately 300 feet from point to point, built of Jurassic sandstone blocks of irregular size, averaging 6 × 8 feet in size.

a) True
b) False

Chapter 6 Review

Dyer and Danforth continue exploring the area. Dyer takes photos of the many strange mural carvings they find and laments that they should have brought more film. Further examination leads the men deeper into the structure, and they note the strange, geometric shapes of the rooms and the fact that they are all bare of portable furnishings. They discover more wall carvings as they search further and assume that the designs are ornamental. They photograph and sketch the various elements they came across, repeatedly encountering a five-pointed-star motif consistent throughout the structure.

When the men come upon an astounding mural that made a profound impression on them, they conclude that the beings who designed this city were neither human nor dinosaurs. They speculated that the creatures must have been extraterrestrial, and their evolution was shaped in the stars.

Discussion Prompts:

1. How does Lovecraft hint at the insignificance and limits of human advancement in this chapter?

2. Dyer calls the mural carvings on walls in the ancient city "mature, accomplished, and aesthetically evolved to the highest degree of civilized mastery." Explain what he means and what moves him to this conclusion.

Chapter Quiz:

6.01. What did Dyer and Danforth use to document their observations after their film was used up?

a) an audio recorder
b) notebook sketches
c) doodles in the snow
d) telegraphs

6.02. What was the condition of the structure that the men entered in the alien city?

a) The building was falling apart.
b) Part of the floor was missing.
c) The structure was well preserved.
d) The roof was missing.

6.03. There were no hints of primordial inscriptions, symbols, or other markings on the unweathered walls of the ancient ruins.

a) True
b) False

6.04. What furnishings did Dyer and Danforth notice in the rooms that they walked through?

a) The rooms were completely empty.
b) only tables
c) discarded wrappers
d) red carpet

6.05. What kind of decorations adorned the walls of the structure which the men entered?

a) photographs
b) flowers
c) wreaths
d) mural sculptures

6.06. How tall were the doorways in the structure?

a) 10 feet
b) 12 feet
c) 13 feet
d) 15 feet

6.07. What advice does Dyer want to convey about further exploration of the Antarctic?

a) It should be discouraged.
b) It should be encouraged because priçeless treasures might be found.
c) Exploration is essential to understanding our own civilization.
d) Exploration would be a waste of time and money.

6.08. Dyer and Danforth soon realized from what the carvings revealed that the alien city was built __________.

a) hundreds of years ago
b) thousands of years ago
c) millions of years ago
d) before the earth was created

6.09. The arabesques displayed a profound use of ________ principles, and were made up of obscurely symmetrical curves and angles based on the quantity of five.

a) geophysical
b) mathematical
c) geographical
d) mechanical

6.10. Dyer believed, based on his observations, that whoever had lived in the alien city eons ago had known that it would have to be evacuated, and its inhabitants had time to prepare.

a) True

b) False

Chapter 7 Review

Dyer theorizes that the mural sculptures they found told of the star-headed beings coming to earth from space. The creatures were able to traverse the sky using their huge wings. They lived under the sea for some time, built fantastic cities, and fought major battles. Dyer believed that the creatures' vast scientific and mechanical knowledge surpassed even that of mankind today. Some sculptures showed that the creatures had lived on other planets, but left because their existence on those worlds was emotionally unfulfilling.

Dyer ascertained that the creatures began their time on earth under the sea. They were able to create food and mold tissue of protoplasmic masses into organs to form slaves, which they then controlled by hypnotic influence to serve their purpose. Dyer believed these fabricated creatures were what the author of a legendary book, the *Necronomicon,* called "shoggoths," and he referred to the creators as the "Old Ones."

Dyer deduces numerous details about the creatures and their time on earth based on the evidence which he and Danforth gather from the murals. He believes another land race shaped like octopi came from the stars at some later time to disrupt the land and create a war. He referred to these creatures as Cthulhu spawn. Eventually, they made peace and new land was given to the Cthulhu spawn, while the Old Ones took to the sea and held on to the older land.

The land above water sank at some point, taking the Cthulhu spawn with it, and the Old Ones that survived reclaimed the land when it eventually resurfaced. The shoggoth seemed to evolve, however, and would become stubborn at times, as if they were developing free will outside of the Old Ones' hypnotic control. A war of re-subjugation apparently erupted between the shoggoth and the Old Ones, who were victorious and managed to regain control of the shoggoth. Dyer likened this to the act of American cowboys taming wild horses.

Evidently, the Old Ones had another interstellar war, this time with an alien race from Pluto that Dyer called Mi-Go. The Mi-Go successfully drove the Old Ones out of all the northern lands and back into their original, Antarctic habitat. Dyer proclaimed that the discoveries the men made in this area would require existing science to be revised, and it gave confirmation to various other scientific hypotheses.

Discussion Prompt:

1. What is Dyer's point of view about the Old Ones' scientific and mechanical knowledge, compared to that of present-day civilization?

Chapter Quiz:

7.01. Where is the full account of Dyer's expedition slated to be published?
a) an official bulletin of Miskatonic University
b) the New York Times
c) a scientific book published by Pabodie
d) None of these answers are correct.

7.02. What book, authored by Abdul Alhazred, does Dyer reference?
a) The Holy Bible
b) The Gypsy King
c) How to be a Millionaire
d) The Necronomicon

7.03. What did the Old Ones who lived in the water apparently have at the end of their tentacles?
a) flaps
b) fur
c) eyes
d) fingers

7.04. How were the Old Ones able to write under the sea?
a) using bubble projectors
b) using a stylus on waterproof, waxed surfaces
c) by tearing off the corners of the vegetation
d) drawing pictures in the sand
e) All of these answers are correct.

7.05. Few of the Old Ones ever died, but in the case of those who did, what caused their demise?
a) old age
b) drug addiction
c) malnutrition
d) violence

7.06. What did the Old Ones use to cover their dead?
a) intricate wreaths
b) woven blankets and favored possessions
c) sticks and leaves
d) five-pointed inscribed mounds
e) All of these answers are correct.

7.07. How did the Old Ones reproduce?

a) mitosis
b) spores
c) hypnosis
d) migration

7.08. How did the land creatures prefer their food?

a) cooked
b) raw
c) frozen
d) crushed into puree

7.09. What temperature was required for the water creatures to survive?

a) boiling
b) 50 degrees
c) freezing
d) 55 degrees

7.10. What did the creatures use for currency?

a) seeds
b) small soapstones
c) emeralds and rubies
d) gold and silver nuggets

7.11. Some of the more recent sculptures depicted a primitive mammal that was sometimes used for food, but also used for what other purpose?

a) decoration
b) furniture
c) amusement
d) ink supply

7.12. What was the name of the stone city built by the Cthulhu spawn?

a) Hartford
b) M'reth
c) Arkham
d) R'lyeh

7.13. On land, the Old Ones used the pseudo-feet, but occasionally, they flew with their wings to great heights and over long distances.

a) True
b) False

7.14. How long ago was the war between the shoggoth and the Old Ones fought?

a) 1,000 years ago
b) 100,00 years ago
c) 150 million years ago
d) None of these answers are correct.

7.15. During what age did the Old Ones undergo another invasion from outer space?

a) the Ophilific Age
b) the Jurassic Age
c) the Gransen Age
d) the Orthopedic Age

7.16. From what planet did the fungoid crustacean invaders originate?

a) Mars
b) Pluto
c) Mercury
d) Saturn

7.17. What were the invading creatures from Pluto called?

a) Mi-Go
b) amigos
c) mitos
d) aliens

Chapter 8 Review

Danforth and Dyer continue their investigation and find a dwelling with decadent sculptures, which helps them deduce more about the history of the region. Dyer becomes convinced that their present location was the fabled nightmare plateau of Leng from the *Necronomicon*. The men notice that some carvings hint at mountains even taller than the Himalayas. The Old Ones had shunned that towering mountainous region as evil., and the cities they had built there eons ago had been left deserted.

Many of the ancient wall sculptures told of a massive river deep under the earth. Something in the water that washed down from the west had caused the Old Ones to recoil, but the particulars of that evil was never depicted in their wall designs. After further investigation, however, Dyer and Danforth got a significant clue about the final calamity that devastated this area from the ruins of a dwelling they were exploring. The carvings showed inhabitants adapting to the need to wear garments to protect themselves from extreme, frigid temperatures. The sculptures also began to depict methods of heating the dwellings. The Old Ones began migrating down to the great river beneath the earth to resume an underwater existence once again, and they built a new city within that cavernous sea. The carvings showed vegetation withering as the region grew colder and the summer snow no longer melted. Dyer was left with no doubt that the cold brought an end to this alien city.

Discussion Prompts:

1. Explain in your own words why the Old Ones left the mountains and returned to living underwater.

2. What is Lovecraft's reason for keeping the description of the "alien monstrosity" subtle throughout the story. For example, Dyer notes that the evil is never depicted on the walls of the aliens' structures.

Chapter Quiz:

8.01. What was the last structure Dyer and Danforth investigated in detail?

a) a trainyard
b) a house
c) a laboratory
d) a laundromat

8.02. The shoggoths conversed with the Old Ones by mimicking their voices.

a) True
b) False

8.03. Dyer said this place was certainly the "strangest, weirdest, and most __________ of all the corners of the earth's globe."

a) terrible
b) robust
c) bleak
d) deadly

8.04. How high were the tallest mountains depicted in the carvings?

a) 25,000 feet
b) 35,000 feet
c) just under 75,000 feet
d) over 40,000 feet

8.05. Why was the expedition unable to see the tallest mountains?

a) The mountains were covered with a haze.
b) The mountains were too far away.
c) The mountains were actually a mirage.
d) The mountains were the same color as the sky.

8.06. Dyer and Danforth discovered that the alien city was built on top of:

a) a cemetery
b) a water source
c) an old hunting ground
d) a volcano

8.07. How long ago did the general glacial periods start?

a) 50,000 years ago
b) 500,000 years ago
c) 5 million years ago

8.08. For what purpose did the Old Ones use shoggoth tissue?

a) to breed stone-lifters
b) holiday recipes
c) decoration
d) fertilizer

8.09. What did Danforth and Dyer agree to remain silent about?

a) the incredible secrets of primal nature
b) the lack of beds and chairs in any of the dwelling structures
c) the contraband artifacts they brought back from the Antarctic
d) the utter injustice of humanity

8.10. With the help of murals, Dyer and Danforth compiled a guide map for navigating their way through the ancient city.

a) True
b) False

8.11. The murals revealed that the Old Ones' dwelling and other structures were linked by __________.

a) doors
b) bridges
c) tunnels
d) elevators

8.12. The Old Ones withdrew from the land and built their new city underwater to escape the unbearably hot, dry weather above ground.

a) True
b) False

8.13. Dyer and Danforth came to know the story of the Old Ones' civilization and eventual extinction from __________.

a) decadent cartouches and dadoes
b) handwritten journals and papyrus maps
c) etchings in sea caverns deep under the earth
d) fossils and other artifacts unearthed on icy mountain slopes

8.14. The pictograms or cartouches on the walls confirmed that as the region grew colder, the Old Ones' livestock and other mammals in the area thrived.

a) True
b) False

Chapter 9 Review

After deducing that a water source existed deep under the Old Ones' mountain city, Dyer and Danforth feel compelled to remain and explore further in the hope of locating it. Darkness engulfed the city, and they agreed to limit their torch use to ensure that they would have sufficient fuel to find their way back. Advancing further also meant that they would have to move swiftly and not stop to examine every wall mural Along the way. Instead, they would focus on locating the water source.

The men progressed through the structures, and soon they became aware of a noxious odor. Dyer recognized that it was the same stench they had encountered in the grave from which Lake had excavated the remains of a long-dead creature to dissect. The men were cautious but intrigued and felt they had come too far to leave without investigating further.

As they moved deeper into the alien labyrinth, Danforth noticed changes in the debris on the ground, suggesting that someone or something had tracked through the area recently. Then, the smell of petrol filled the air. They whispered about the possible connection between Lake's ransacked camp and what they might find if they forge ahead, ultimately deciding that they must advance. They did so with great caution but soon found that their path was blocked and they would have to find another route.

As they passed through a doorway and entered an adjoining room, the smell of petrol grew stronger. Inside, they discovered a freshly abandoned campsite, left behind by unknown intruders whom they presumed might have been exploring but were turned back by the blocked entry to the underground abyss. Upon a closer inspection, Dyer and Danforth found several scattered objects that caused alarm—they appeared to be the missing items pilfered from Lake's camp site. They also found curiously inked sketches on paper in the unmistakable marking techniques of the Old Ones. They examined the drawings and then retraced their steps back the way they came, intending to follow a path indicated in one of the sketches that evidently led to an enormous round structure.

After some time, they reached the cylindrical area and found more items from Lake's camp. Three sledges had been tucked away out of view, along with other items taken from the camp. Upon lifting an oddly shaped tarpaulin, they discovered the frozen, perfectly preserved bodies of Gedney and the missing dog.

Discussion Prompts:

1. What effect does Lovecraft try to achieve by showing readers the frozen, preserved remains of Gedney and the dog at the end of the chapter?

2. How would you compare Lake's attempt to dissect the frozen remains of the alien creatures that his expedition had unearthed with the Old Ones' attempt to preserve human bodies in ice?

Chapter Quiz:

9.01. What time was it when Dyer and Danforth decided to look for the water source during their survey of the ancient city?

a) 3 a.m.
b) 8 a.m.
c) 8 p.m.
d) 10 p.m.

9.02. Who first noticed the familiar stench of alien death in the air of the area being explored?

a) Gedney
b) Danforth
c) Dyer
d) Pabodie

9.03. What strange odor did the men smell inside the Cyclopean burial place during their survey?

a) burnt flesh
b) petrol
c) floral fragrance
d) mildew

9.04. What conclusion did Dyer and Danforth jump to when they detected the smell of petrol?

a) They were certain that an ancient gas station was nearby.
b) They wondered if someone was cooking.
c) They assumed that their airplane had been stolen and hidden nearby.
d) They believed there was a connection between the horrors at Lake's camp and whatever menace was ahead of them in the cavern.

9.05. What shocking discovery did the men make when they looked under the tarpaulin on the partly obscured sledge?

a) the bodies of Gedney and the missing dog
b) a shoggoth's disintegrated corpse
c) the intact, perfectly preserved body of an Old One
d) a handwritten note that said "GET OUT!"
e) None of these answers are correct.

9.06. What did Danforth think he saw in the debris while he and Dyer were surveying cavern?
a) lead shavings
b) parallel tracks
c) bare footprints
d) unearthly blue sparkles

9.07. As they made their way through the ancient ruins, Dyer and Danforth discovered that their route to the tunnel which they believed led to a vast underground river was blocked, so they had to find a different route.
a) True
b) False

9.08. What drove Dyer and Danforth to continue moving deeper into the alien city?
a) burning curiosity
b) anxiety
c) a sense of responsibility toward Gedney
d) All of these answers are correct.

9.09. What did the searchers find in the corner of one room during their survey of the catacombs?
a) a massive tangle of spider webs
b) a considerable amount of spilled gasoline
c) a small pile of petrified fruit
d) a box of weapons of a design they had never seen before

9.10. What else did Dyer and Danforth find in the room which they accessed through the tunnel?
a) spent matches
b) a broken fountain pen
c) three illustrated books
d) All of these answers are correct.

9.11. What did the searchers see at 9:30 p.m. as they made their way through the abandoned tunnel?
a) daylight
b) the moon
c) a gigantic, circular spaceship
d) a device quite similar to a portable radio

Chapter 10 Review

After recovering from the shock of their discovery, Dyer and Danforth hear a strange sound nearby. They soon realize that it is the squawking of a bird. Surprised to encounter such a life form in this bitterly cold environment, they search for the source and come upon a huge, eyeless albino penguin. They decide to follow the penguin tracks further into the abyss.

As they proceed, they notice curious changes in the wall murals. The artistry is quite different, as if the graceful engravings of the Old Ones had been degraded, their finely crafted symbols replaced with crude attempts at replication. The men knew that they could not spend time studying the murals, so they continued on.

Before long, Dyer and Danforth encounter a new and unfamiliar smell and discover a new obstruction in their path. They did not think it was a penguin, but nevertheless, ignoring the likelihood of danger from unseen and unknown creatures, they move ahead after assuring themselves that whatever it was laying before them was not moving.

Discussion Prompt:

1. What is Lovecraft suggesting to readers when he reveals that the fresh carvings on the wall are similar to the Old Ones' art but had a crude quality to them?

Chapter Quiz:

10.01. What sound did the men hear in the cavern?

a) water dripping
b) the howl of a coyote
c) a penguin squawking
d) terrifying whispers of the dead

10.02. What color was the eyeless penguin that the men encountered?

a) black
b) green
c) brown
d) white

10.03. Dyer observed that the more recent carvings in the passages around them were coarse, bold, and lacked the graceful detail that they had seen previously in the Old Ones' engravings.

a) True
b) False

10.04. How tall did Dyer and Danforth estimate the huge penguin to be?
a) 2 feet tall
b) 3 feet tall
c) 5 feet tall
d) 6 feet tall

10.05. What other items from the camp did the men encounter as their survey took them deeper into the ruins?
a) notebooks and journals
b) dishes to eat on
c) cans of tuna fish
d) furs cut to fit bizarre shapes

10.06. What did the men follow as they tracked the albino penguin?
a) a strange light source
b) penguin droppings
c) the sound of rushing water
d) a map

10.07. How many torches were Dyer and Danforth using at this point?
a) two
b) four
c) six
d) eight

10.08. The perpetual darkness of the warmer inner region had destroyed the penguins' pigmentation and atrophied their eyes to useless slits.
a) True
b) False

10.09. Dyer and Danforth were able to take several clear photos of the giant penguins in the caverns.
a) True
b) False

10.10. The cavern formed by the artificial destruction of walls between the honeycombing had __________.
a) a polished and glistening floor
b) massive piles of debris which buried the floor
c) a floor with enormous cracks and gaping holes
d) None of these answers are correct.

Chapter 11 Review

Dyer and Danforth realize that the obstruction in their path is what they feared most: the objects were life forms, like the hideous creatures found partially intact at Lake's camp. The creatures' bodies have been mutilated, and they are quite dead. As the men examine the remains, they observe a disgusting green ichor oozing from multiple injuries, including decapitation. Danforth screams in terror as he sees bubbling, black slime exuding from one of the entities that inflicted this horrific carnage, and they recognize the hideous being from the drawings that they had seen all over the ancient city—it was a shoggoth. The vile creature was part of a band that had brutally attacked and killed the Old Ones, whose corpses were strewn across the ground, just as the murals depicted in the history of the earlier re-subjugation war. The men reacted in horror at a nearby sound that finally convinced them to turn and flee from this terrible place. When they had returned to safety, and when they looked back on that terrifying sound, they realized it was a sound from a writing by Poe—a sound that came from the great, spectral, snowy birds he had described in a book.

Danforth's piercing scream had caught the attention of a shoggoth that had stopped to examine a fallen comrade, and it began pursuit as the men turned to run. The penguins in the vicinity were clearly alarmed and darted frantically about squawking. The men ran for their lives, doubting that they would be able to escape their vile pursuer and the ruins around them that entombed a once-powerful alien race. Abject terror left Danforth unstrung, and Dyer later heard him chanting the names of train stations from the Boston Cambridge tunnel. Except they were not at a train station, and the hulking image of a fast-approaching shoggoth that comminated their senses was much more terrifying than an onrushing subway train.

Discussion Prompts

1. What shocking discovery did Dyer and Danforth make when they encountered a massive obstruction in their path?

2. Why did Danforth beginning chanting the names of train stations in America as he and Dyer fled from the onrushing shoggoth?

Chapter Quiz

11.01. How many dead creatures did the men find in the caverns during their survey?

a) two
b) four
c) nine

11.02. What body part was missing from some of the Old Ones who had been slaughtered by the shoggoth?

a) their heads
b) their hands
c) their feet
d) their arms

11.03. How did Danforth react to discovering the source of the horrible stench in the cavern?

a) He took off running.
b) He froze in his tracks.
c) He screamed.
d) He cursed several times.

11.04. Who or what had slaughtered the four Old Ones that Dyer and Danforth came upon?

a) a warring rival gang of Old Ones
b) shoggoth
c) rabid penguins
d) Gedney

11.05. What sound prompted Dyer and Danforth to finally abandon their survey and frantically retreat from the abyss?

a) the penguins' footsteps
b) someone crying
c) a faint humming
d) the repeated word, *Tekeli-li! Tekeli-li!*

11.06. What was Danforth chanting as he fled from the pursuing shoggoth?

a) an incantation from the *Necronomicon*
b) the names of train stations
c) a poem by Edgar Allen Poe
d) his home address and phone number

11.07. What was making the *Tekeli-li Tekeli-li* sound that terrified Dyer and Danforth?

a) penguins
b) an aeroplane
c) a shoggoth
d) the age-old ice breaking underfoot

11.08. How were the Old Ones' heads decapitated by the shoggoth?

a) clean laceration
b) with deliberate precision
c) whacked off by a primitive knife or sword
d) tearing or suction

11.09. The Old Ones' heads had the shape of a __________.

a) rectangle
b) starfish
c) triangle
d) snake

11.10. A noxious, black, tar-like substance oozed onto the ground around the Old Ones' mutilated bodies.

a) True
b) False

11.11. The frightened squawking and frantic darting about of the penguins helped Dyer and Danforth escape by distracting the shoggoth.

a) True
b) False

Chapter 12 Review

Dyer and Danforth are fatigued as they struggle up the colossal spire and flee from the depths below. They did not discuss what they had witnessed or heard that caused them to retreat from the alien city. When they reached the plane, they stopped to catch their breath and glanced back at the violet panorama of the Antarctic landscape beyond. They could see the explored lands of the tallest mountains and realized that they were the first humans ever to view this remarkable sight. Inexplicably, those mountains seemed even more foreboding than the grotesque terrors they had just survived, and Dyer hoped that his expedition would be the last to lay eyes on this remote, hostile wasteland at the earth's southern pole.

Once on board the plane, they pulled on their furs and made a smooth takeoff. However, Danforth became so disturbed while piloting the plane that Dyer offered to take over the controls. They switched positions, but Danforth remained highly agitated. Suddenly, he saw something that provoked a terrible shriek. He refused to talk about what he saw, and to this day, he will not speak of it.

In recounting the story of the ill-fated expedition, Dyer implores the Starkweather-Moore party to heed his warning and abandon their planned expedition to the Antarctic, insisting, "It is absolutely necessary for the peace and safety of mankind." The story ends with Danforth shrieking in a fit of madness and repeating over and over, *Tekeli-li! Tekeli-li!*

Discussion Prompts

1. How does Lovecraft portray the exploration and conquest of far-off continents by men of science in this story?

2. How does the story's ending challenge our present-day notions of time, space, and life on planet earth?

3. Why is Danforth reduced to unintelligible babbling in the last chapter of the story? Is the human mind incapable of comprehending the deepest secrets of the universe? Explain your rationale.

Chapter Quiz

12.01. After their escape from the alien city, what time was it when Dyer and Danforth reached the safety of their plane?

a) midnight
b) early in the morning
c) noon
d) lunchtime

12.02. Approximately how far away was the towering mountain range that Dyer and Danforth were the first humans to see at the end of the story?
a) 100 miles
b) 150 miles
c) 200 miles
d) 300 miles

12.03. The foreboding slopes of the ancient mountains that engulfed the Old Ones' lost city reminded Dyer and Danforth of paintings by this artist:
a) Vincent Van Gogh
b) Edgar Allen Poe
c) Sabastian Bach
d) Nicholas Roerich

12.04. Who started the airplane after Dyer and Danforth escaped from the monstrous shoggoth pursuing them and fled from the alien city?
a) Dyer
b) Danforth
c) Pabodie
d) Gedney

12.05. As they prepared to take off from the icy mountain slope and return to the base camp, Dyer noticed that Danforth was badly shaken following their harrowing experience in the alien city and offered him a swig of whiskey to calm his nerves.
a) True
b) False

12.06. What did Dyer and Danforth discuss on their flight to the base camp?
a) who would win the next U.S. presidential election
b) the events and observations that they would keep secret
c) what they would do on their first night back in America
d) how the huge penguins managed to survive the bitter Antarctic weather

12.07. What book is kept under lock and key in the library at Miskatonic University?
a) a notebook of employees' addresses and phone numbers
b) a book containing photographs from the Antarctic expedition
c) The *Necronomicon*
d) a ledger containing contracts and other financial arrangements that funded Dyer's expedition to the Antarctic

12.08. What did Danforth hint that he saw in his final horror that pushed him over the edge into madness?

a) a masked intruder
b) a killer penguin
c) a blood-red sea
d) a mirage

12.09. What did Danforth shriek after he saw the Old Ones' mutilated remains in the ruins of the alien city?

a) Stop!
b) Run!
c) Tekeli-li
d) Help!

12.10. What does Danforth whisper about in his fits of madness?

a) the black pit
b) the proto-shoggoths
c) the moon-ladder
d) All of these answers are correct.

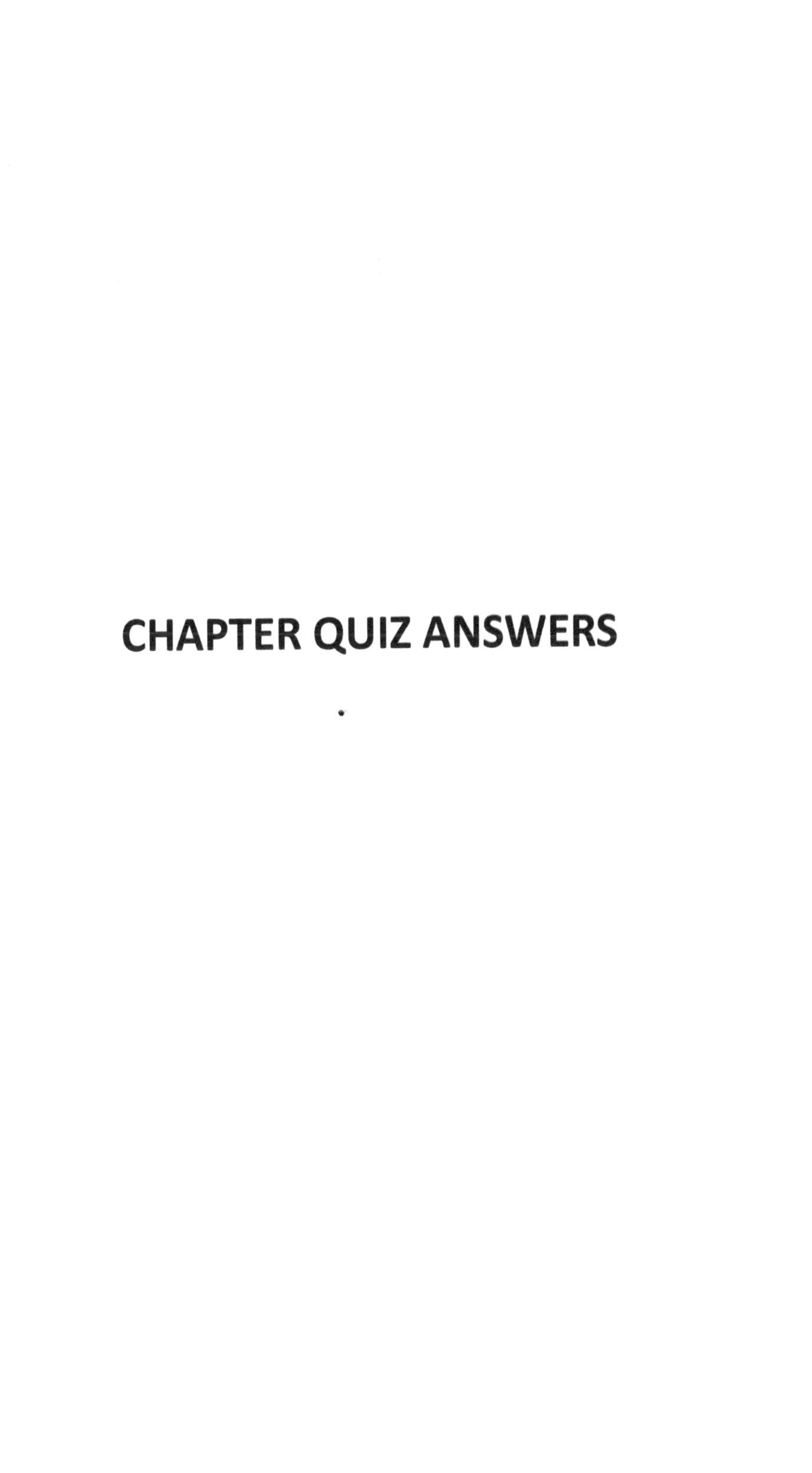

CHAPTER QUIZ ANSWERS

Chapter 1 Quiz Answers

1.01. The narrator of this story is Professor __________.
b) Dyer

1.02. Which university is the narrator of the story affiliated with?
c) Miskatonic University

1.03. What is the narrator's profession?
a) geologist

1.04. The Miskatonic expedition's destination is __________.
a) mountains in the Antarctic

1.05. Who developed the new drilling equipment that the expedition hopes will help them make discoveries about the region's distant past?
c) Prof. Pabodie

1.06. What features made Pabodie's new drilling apparatus noteworthy?
d) All of these answers are correct.

1.07. How many airplanes were needed to transport the expedition?
c) four

1.08. How many sledges were needed to pull the drilling apparatus over the icy tundra?
b) three

1.09. What did the Pabodie Expedition hope to find during its trip to the frozen continent of Antarctica?
c) materials that would explain more about the earth's past

1.10. How many assistants participated in the Miskatonic expedition?
c) sixteen

1.11. How was the Pabodie Expedition financed?
a) Nathaniel Derby Pickman Foundation

1.12. What date did the expedition embark on its journey?
d) September 2, 1930

1.13. Had anyone on the Pabodie Expedition visited the Antarctic before?
a) only the ship captains

1.14. What was the date that the expedition caught a glimpse of land as they approached their destination?
d) October 26

1.15. When was the expedition finally able to set foot on land?
b) November 8

1.16. What great poet does Danforth evoke when he sees lava on a snowy slope?
a) Edgar Allen Poe

1.17. When did the expedition arrive at Ross Island?
a) shortly after midnight

1.18. The expedition's base ship was named __________.
b) The Arkham

1.19. What is the name of the second ship in the Pabodie Expedition?
c) The Miskatonic

1.20. How many dogs accompanied the expedition on their journey?
a) 55 Alaskan sledge dogs

1.21. How tall is Mount Nansen?
c) 15,000 feet

1.22. Who ascended Mt. Nansen with Prof. Pabodie on Dec. 13-15?
a) Gedney and Carroll

1.23. What did the expedition members drink to offset the steady diet of tinned and salted food?
a) lime juice

1.24. When the expedition discovered oddly marked fragments, how old did they estimate these artifacts to be?
c) 500 million years

Chapter 2 Quiz Answers

2.01. When did Lake's party do their preliminary sledging and boring?
d) January 11-18

2.02. How many dogs were lost during Lake's excursion?
a) two

2.03. How many men accompanied Lake on his excursion?
a) seven

2.04. What did the narrator of the story say it was unwise to be without?
c) transportation

2.05. On what date did Lake make his most exciting discovery?
d) January 22

2.06. What time was the first wireless message from Lake received?
a) 6:00 a.m.

2.07. How far away was Lake's drilling site from Dyer's base camp?
a) 300 miles

2.08. During Lake's flight, what observation did he make at 10:05 p.m.?
c) a large mountain range

2.09. What bad news did Lake relay from his camp around 10:05 p.m.?
b) Moulton's plane was forced down on a plateau.

2.10. Where did Lake decide to camp while the downed plane was being repaired?
a) at the location where it went down

2.11. What environmental factors worried Lake during his flight?
b) the heavy winds

2.12. What covered the roof and floor of the cave that Lake discovered?
a) stalactites and stalagmites

2.13. What geological age did Lake conclude the newest fossils in the cave were from?

d) the Oligocene Age

2.14. During Lake's journey, he sent out a series of communications. What was the substance of these messages?

a) details about the fossils they were finding

2.15. To whom did Lake want to convey the importance of his scientific findings?

b) the press

2.16. How many barrel specimens did Lake's expedition unearth?

b) fourteen

2.17. When did Lake plan to dissect one of the creatures he had excavated?

c) as soon as they got back to camp

2.18. What color was the thick fluid that oozed from the creature?

a) green

2.19. How many lobes did Lake observe in the creature's brain?

b) five

Chapter 3 Quiz Answers

3.01. How many planes escorted Lake on his doomed sub-expedition?
a) four

3.02. How many hours of sleep did the men at the base camp get before they went out to search for Lake?
d) four

3.03. On what date did Dyer's party go out searching for Lake's group?
b) January 25

3.04. How many dogs did the search party bring to Lake's camp?
c) seven

3.05. What was the weather on the morning that the search party set out for Lake's camp?
d) All of these answers are correct.

3.06. How long did it take the rescuers to reach Lake's camp?
b) four and a half hours

3.07. Why was the rescue flight in this chapter burned into Dyer's memory?
c) It marked the loss of his sense of peace and balance.

3.08. What name did Dyer give to the dark spires that he saw?
c) mountains of madness

3.09. How did Dyer describe what the mountain slopes overlooked?
a) some accursed ultimate abyss

3.10. Why did Dyer recount this story despite his vow to keep it secret?
b) He wanted to warn others.

3.11. How many of the dogs that accompanied Lake's party survived?
c) none

3.12. How many intact specimens remained at Lake's outpost when Dyer and the other searchers arrived?
a) none

3.13. Why was Dyer so careful about the wording in his relays to the *Arkham*?

a) He did not want to alarm the public.

3.14. What did Danforth think he saw on the scouting tour with Dyer?

b) He has never told anyone what he saw.

3.15. What were the two ships that would take the expedition back to the United States?

d) the Arkham and the Miskatonic

3.16. Which character from the story had a nervous breakdown upon returning to the U.S.?

b) Danforth

3.17. What is the name of the expedition party that intends to undertake a follow-up trip to Antarctica?

c) Starkweather-Moore expedition

Chapter 4 Quiz Answers

4.01. Professor Dyer was an expert when it came to flying a plane.
b) False

4.02. When thcy counted the remains of the dead dogs, how many were missing?
a) one

4.03. Whose body was missing when Dyer and Danforth performed the search?
b) Gedney

4.04. Where were most of the bodies found during the search of Lake's camp?
d) in one of the airplane shelters

4.05. What item or items were missing from Lake's dissecting tent?
d) All of these answers are correct.

4.06. What evidence of the gruesome scene at Lake's camp was Dyer able to take back with him?
c) photographs

4.07. What did Dyer plan to do with the horrific evidence gathered at Lake's devastated outpost?
b) show it to the Starkweather-Moore party in the hope that it would dissuade them from returning to the Antarctic

4.08. How high up did the plane take Dyer and Danforth during their aerial search of the area around Lake's outpost?
a) 23,570 feet

4.09. Dyer saw a half-impression of faint snow-prints in one shielded corner of the ruined enclosure during his search.
a) True

4.10. Around the mangled bodies, Dyer found an odd sprinkling of ______, which had been taken from a pillaged provision-chest on the planes.
c) salt

4.11. The covered remains of the primal monstrosity Lake had uncovered had been removed from the makeshift table in the dissecting tent.

a) True

4.12. Pabodie was driven to a nervous collapse by the horrors he had witnessed during the expedition to the Antarctic.

b) False

4.13. After the bodies of Lake's team and the dogs were examined, what did Dyer conclude was the cause of death?

b) strangulation or laceration

4.14. The ancient and wind-weathered rock layers that Dyer's expedition had excavated verified all of Lake's astounding bulletins.

a) True

4.15. Lake's original suspicion of smoking cones did prove to be natural, volcanic structures.

b) False

Chapter 5 Quiz Answers

5.01. How high was the table of land that the expedition found?
a) 20,000 feet

5.02. Before Dyer and Danforth left the rampart, they drew a dozen sketches of the area to document its remarkable, mortarless masonry.
b) False

5.03. Based on the description in this chapter, how tall were the massive stone walls of the labyrinth?
a) 10-150 feet

5.04. What connected many of the towers to one another in the alien city?
d) stone bridges

5.05. What did the expedition conclude had once existed in the bare area that they observed?
c) a river

5.06. What evidence did the men take back with them from the plane trip recounted in this chapter?
b) photographs

5.07. What did the sight of the vast alien city cause Danforth and Dyer to wonder?
a) what sort of beings had built it and who lived there

5.08. What did the men plan to use to help them find their way back out of the cavernous structures that they wanted to enter?
c) shredded paper

5.09. What shape were many of the topographical points of interest that the expedition found?
c) star-shaped

5.10. Who did Dyer and Danforth wish was there to help them?
b) Pabodie

5.11. What covered many of the window structures they found in the city?
d) shutters

5.12. The alien city was badly weather-beaten, and the glacial surface from which the towers projected was strewn with fallen blocks and debris.
a) True

5.13. The rampart was shaped like a star and approximately 300 feet from point to point, built of Jurassic sandstone blocks of irregular size, averaging 6 × 8 feet in size.
a) True

Chapter 6 Quiz Answers

6.01. What did Dyer and Danforth use to document their observations after their film was used up?

b) notebook sketches

6.02. What was the condition of the structure that the men entered in the alien city?

c) The structure was well preserved.

6.03. There were no hints of primordial inscriptions, symbols, or other markings on the unweathered walls of the ancient ruins.

b) False

6.04. What furnishings did Dyer and Danforth notice in the rooms that they walked through?

a) The rooms were completely empty.

6.05. What kind of decorations adorned the walls of the structure which the men entered?

d) mural sculptures

6.06. How tall were the doorways in the structure?

b) 12 feet

6.07. What advice does Dyer want to convey about further exploration of the Antarctic?

a) It should be discouraged.

6.08. Dyer and Danforth soon realized from what the carvings revealed that the alien city was built __________.

c) millions of years ago

6.09. The arabesques displayed a profound use of ________ principles, and were made up of obscurely symmetrical curves and angles based on the quantity of five.

b) mathematical

6.10. Dyer believed, based on his observations, that whoever had lived in the alien city eons ago had known that it would have to be evacuated, and its inhabitants had time to prepare.

a) True

Chapter 7 Quiz Answers

7.01. Where is the full account of Dyer's expedition slated to be published?
a) an official bulletin of Miskatonic University

7.02. What book, authored by Abdul Alhazred, does Dyer reference?
d) The Necronomicon

7.03. What did the Old Ones who lived in the water apparently have at the end of their tentacles?
c) eyes

7.04. How were the Old Ones able to write under the sea?
b) using a stylus on waterproof, waxed surfaces

7.05. Few of the Old Ones ever died, but in the case of those who did, what caused their demise?
d) violence

7.06. What did the Old Ones use to cover their dead?
d) five-pointed inscribed mounds

7.07. How did the Old Ones reproduce?
b) spores

7.08. How did the land creatures prefer their food?
a) cooked

7.09. What temperature was required for the water creatures to survive?
c) freezing

7.10. What did the creatures use for currency?
b) small soapstones

7.11. Some of the more recent sculptures depicted a primitive mammal that was sometimes used for food, but also used for what other purpose?
c) amusement

7.12. What was the name of the stone city built by the Cthulhu spawn?
d) R'lyeh

7.13. On land, the Old Ones used the pseudo-feet, but occasionally, they flew with their wings to great heights and over long distances.
a) True

7.14. How long ago was the war between the shoggoth and the Old Ones fought?
c) 150 million years ago

7.15. During what age did the Old Ones undergo another invasion from outer space?
b) the Jurassic Age

7.16. From what planet did the fungoid crustacean invaders originate?
b) Pluto

7.17. What were the invading creatures from Pluto called?
a) Mi-Go

Chapter 8 Quiz Answers

8.01. What was the last structure Dyer and Danforth investigated in detail?
b) a house

8.02. The shoggoths conversed with the Old Ones by mimicking their voices.
a) True

8.03. Dyer said this place was certainly the "strangest, weirdest, and most __________ of all the corners of the earth's globe."
a) terrible

8.04. How high were the tallest mountains depicted in the carvings?
d) over 40,000 feet

8.05. Why was the expedition unable to see the tallest mountains?
a) The mountains were covered with a haze.

8.06. Dyer and Danforth discovered that the alien city was built on top of:
b) a water source

8.07. How long ago did the general glacial periods start?
b) 500,000 years ago

8.08. For what purpose did the Old Ones use shoggoth tissue?
a) to breed stone-lifters

8.09. What did Danforth and Dyer agree to remain silent about?
a) the incredible secrets of primal nature

8.10. With the help of murals, Dyer and Danforth compiled a guide map for navigating their way through the ancient city.
a) True

8.11. The murals revealed that the Old Ones' dwelling and other structures were linked by __________.
c) tunnels

8.12. The Old Ones withdrew from the land and built their new city underwater to escape the unbearably hot, dry weather above ground.
b) False

8.13. Dyer and Danforth came to know the story of the Old Ones' civilization and eventual extinction from __________.

a) decadent cartouches and dadoes

8.14. The pictograms or cartouches on the walls confirmed that as the region grew colder, the Old Ones' livestock and other mammals in the area thrived.

b) False

Chapter 9 Quiz Answers

9.01. What time was it when Dyer and Danforth decided to look for the water source during their survey of the ancient city?
c) 8 p.m.

9.02. Who first noticed the familiar stench of alien death in the air of the area being explored?
b) Danforth

9.03. What strange odor did the men smell inside the Cyclopean burial place during their survey?
b) petrol

9.04. What conclusion did Dyer and Danforth jump to when they detected the smell of petrol?
d) They believed there was a connection between the horrors at Lake's camp and whatever menace was ahead of them in the cavern.

9.05. What shocking discovery did the men make when they looked under the tarpaulin on the partly obscured sledge?
a) the bodies of Gedney and the missing dog

9.06. What did Danforth think he saw in the debris while he and Dyer were surveying cavern?
b) parallel tracks

9.07. As they made their way through the ancient ruins, Dyer and Danforth discovered that their route to the tunnel which they believed led to a vast underground river was blocked, so they had to find a different route.
a) True

9.08. What drove Dyer and Danforth to continue moving deeper into the alien city?
d) All of these answers are correct.

9.09. What did the searchers find in the corner of one room during their survey of the catacombs?
b) a considerable amount of spilled gasoline

9.10. What else did Dyer and Danforth find in the room which they accessed through the tunnel?

d) All of these answers are correct.

9.11. What did the searchers see at 9:30 p.m. as they made their way through the abandoned tunnel?

a) daylight

Chapter 10 Quiz Answers

10.01. What sound did the men hear in the cavern?
c) a penguin squawking

10.02. What color was the eyeless penguin that the men encountered?
d) white

10.03. Dyer observed that the more recent carvings in the passages around them were coarse, bold, and lacked the graceful detail that they had seen previously in the Old Ones' engravings.
a) True

10.04. How tall did Dyer and Danforth estimate the huge penguin to be?
d) 6 feet tall

10.05. What other items from the camp did the men encounter as their survey took them deeper into the ruins?
d) furs cut to fit bizarre shapes

10.06. What did the men follow as they tracked the albino penguin?
b) penguin droppings

10.07. How many torches were Dyer and Danforth using at this point?
a) two

10.08. The perpetual darkness of the warmer inner region had destroyed the penguins' pigmentation and atrophied their eyes to useless slits.
a) True

10.09. Dyer and Danforth were able to take several clear photos of the giant penguins in the caverns.
b) False

10.10. The cavern formed by the artificial destruction of walls between the honeycombing had __________.
a) a polished and glistening floor

Chapter 11 Quiz Answers

11.01. How many dead creatures did the men find in the caverns during their survey?
b) four

11.02. What body part was missing from some of the Old Ones who had been slaughtered by the shoggoth?
a) their heads

11.03. How did Danforth react to discovering the source of the horrible stench in the cavern?
c) He screamed.

11.04. Who or what had slaughtered the four Old Ones that Dyer and Danforth came upon?
b) shoggoth

11.05. What sound prompted Dyer and Danforth to finally abandon their survey and frantically retreat from the abyss?
d) the repeated word, *Tekeli-li! Tekeli-li!*

11.06. What was Danforth chanting as he fled from the pursuing shoggoth?
b) the names of train stations

11.07. What was making the *Tekeli-li Tekeli-li* sound that terrified Dyer and Danforth?
c) a shoggoth

11.08. How were the Old Ones' heads decapitated by the shoggoth?
d) tearing or suction

11.09. The Old Ones' heads had the shape of a __________.
b) starfish

11.10. A noxious, black, tar-like substance oozed onto the ground around the Old Ones' mutilated bodies.
b) False

11.11. The frightened squawking and frantic darting about of the penguins helped Dyer and Danforth escape by distracting the shoggoth.
a) True

Chapter 12 Quiz Answers

12.01. After their escape from the alien city, what time was it when Dyer and Danforth reached the safety of their plane?
a) midnight

12.02. Approximately how far away was the towering mountain range that Dyer and Danforth were the first humans to see at the end of the story?
d) 300 miles

12.03. The foreboding slopes of the ancient mountains that engulfed the Old Ones' lost city reminded Dyer and Danforth of paintings by this artist:
d) Nicholas Roerich

12.04. Who started the airplane after Dyer and Danforth escaped from the monstrous shoggoth pursuing them and fled from the alien city?
b) Danforth

12.05. As they prepared to take off from the icy mountain slope and return to the base camp, Dyer noticed that Danforth was badly shaken following their harrowing experience in the alien city and offered him a swig of whiskey to calm his nerves.
b) False

12.06. What did Dyer and Danforth discuss on their flight to the base camp?
b) the events and observations that they would keep secret

12.07. What book is kept under lock and key in the library at Miskatonic University?
c) The Necronomicon

12.08. What did Danforth hint that he saw in his final horror that pushed him over the edge into madness?
d) a mirage

12.09. What did Danforth shriek after he saw the Old Ones' mutilated remains in the ruins of the alien city?
c) Tekeli-li

12.10. What does Danforth whisper about in his fits of madness?
d) All of these answers are correct.

www.ingramcontent.com/pod-product-compliance
Lightning Source LLC
Chambersburg PA
CBHW030413310726
48979CB00002B/401

* 9 7 8 1 6 4 3 9 9 0 3 0 9 *